Nothing
is
EASY

By Donna Schlachter
and
Leeann Betts

Book 4 in the
Mysterious Ink Mystery
Bookstore series

© 2021

ISBN: 978-1-943688-84-5
Published by: PLS Bookworks,
Denver, CO

DEDICATION

First and foremost, to God the Father, Jesus the Son, and
The Holy Spirit, the Godhead, three in one.
Without them, no story is worth telling.

To my pen name, Leeann Betts. Born from a desire
not to confuse my readers, when in fact,
I didn't give you enough credit.
Lee is my husband's middle name, *Ann* is
his mother's middle name,
And *Betts* was my mother's name in nursing school.
Leeann happily retires as of this book, but I will continue
to write stories she'd be proud to put her name on.

To my faithful readers: without you, writing stories
wouldn't be as much fun. Thanks!

Books By Leeann Betts:

By the Numbers series featuring Carly Turnquist, forensic accountant

No Accounting for Murder	Petty Cash
There Was a Crooked Man	A Deadly Dissolution
Unbalanced	Silent Partner
Five and Twenty Blackbirds	In the Money
Broke, Busted, and Disgusted	Missing Deposits
Hidden Assets	Risk Management

Mysterious Ink Bookstore series featuring Margie Hanson, librarian

The Game is Afoot
Little Grey Cells
Heavier Than Broken Hearts
Co-Authored with Donna Schlachter
Nothing is Easy

The Worst-Kept Secret in "Always a Wedding Planner" Collection"

Counting the Days: a 31-day devotional
In Search of Christmas Past – a novel

By Leeann and Donna:

Nuggets of Writing Gold -- articles and essays on writing.
More Nuggets of Writing Gold – more articles and essays on writing

Books by Donna Schlachter:

Mended by God series –healing & wholeness for heart & soul
Broken Dreams, Mended Heart
Broken Dreams, Mended Family
Broken Dreams, Mended Marriage

I Do – Again: a devotional for remarrieds

Second Chances and Second Cups: A short story collection.
The Physics of Love
The Mystery of Christmas Inn, Colorado
Christmas Under the Stars
Transformation – a devotional

Time Will Tell – Christmas Under Main Street series

The Oregon Trail Mysteries series
Kate
A Pink Lady Thanksgiving

Healing the Wounded Heart series
Testing Tessa
Justice for Julia

Written in Love series: *Cactus Lil and the City Slicker*

Hearts of the Pony Express series: *Hollenberg Hearts*

Mail-Order Brides series: *The New Hope Train*

Available at Online Retailers and Fine Booksellers:
Quiet Moments Alone with God: a devotional
100 Answers to 100 Questions About Loving Your Husband
Double Jeopardy: a novel about murder, mining, and a mock marriage
Detours of the Heart – MISSadventure Brides Romance Collection

Chapter 1

With Thanksgiving but a memory in her rearview mirror, Margie Hanson looked ahead to Christmas at her bookstore in downtown Edgewater, Colorado. Her guide dog trainee, JoJo, lay at her feet behind the register on this quiet Monday.

She nibbled on the end of the candy cane she'd plucked from the cup on the counter. The treat intended for customers. Of which she had none. Not a surprise. She didn't open on Mondays. A respite after the previous busy week, full Sunday at church and dinner with Ed Hogan, the special man in her life right now. Who asked her on Thanksgiving Day to marry him. Had she made the correct choice? He'd assured her he had no qualms about her continuing to operate her store.

"Think, Margie. You can come up with a good idea for Christmas." Another nibble. Time to roll the plastic wrapper down an inch or so. "Maybe I should put everything on sale." She glanced down at the black Labrador, who raised her head and snorted. "You're right. That would look tacky. And desperate."

Still, generating additional cash flow sat number one on her goals. If she stood any chance of completing the addition to her store—without selling her soul to the devil or the banker—she needed a lot of cash.

Her first edition of *The Adventure of the Grange*, featuring Sherlock Holmes, stared up at her from the locked display case that also served as register stand and customer contact point. She could sell that—along with a couple of other books from the case—and cover her renovations. She shook her head. Simply considering that possibility gave her the creeps. Those books were not for sale—at any price. For any reason.

No way. No how.

She exhaled. Then again, she could likely find replacements—no. She must hold some things— including her faith, her family, JoJo, and her vintage manuscripts—apart from the world.

But maybe she could feature those books as examples of great mysteries. Sell modern-day copies. Have contests and drawings. A scavenger hunt, of sorts, throughout the store, where customers could discover other exceptional stories.

A Christmas Mystery Event. Something for everybody.

Just what she needed. An event and an engagement party to plan.

She ran her engagement ring up and down the chain she kept hidden beneath her shirt. Wanting to keep the big reveal a secret until the party, they'd decided she could wear the ring, but not in public. However, the emerald-cut diamond solitaire was simply too gorgeous to

8

leave shut up in its box for two more weeks.

Wait. Could she combine the two events? The finale of the Christmas mystery event and the announcement? After all, most of her friends were customers. And most of her customers were friends. Living in a small town tended to overlap and blur the lines of relationship. Which almost got her into hot water when she first arrived. Thank goodness Grandma Carly accompanied her on that new adventure.

A knock at the front door drew her attention. Ed Hogan, detective with the Edgewater Police Department and her fiancé, cupped his hands around his eyes, peered through the glass, and smiled at her.

She slid off the stool, crossed the retail area, and unlocked the door. "Just in time."

"That's what I like to hear." His rumpled overcoat confirmed the chilly temperatures outside. "Always like to help a damsel in distress."

She accepted a kiss on the cheek. "I wouldn't go that far. Just need some brainstorming."

He groaned. "The engagement party?"

"No."

"I already said we didn't need that. Let's just line up the best man and the maid of honor and elope."

She laughed and mock-punched his shoulder. "Not going to happen. My parents would kill us."

He waggled his eyebrows. "We'd die happy."

Another punch. "You look exactly like my grandpa when you do that."

9

"Nah, he's too old for that stuff."

She chuckled. "I hope we're never too old."

"True." He scratched his chin. "What's the topic?"

"A fun event to bring customers into the shop."

He leaned on the case and drew a circle in the dust accumulating from the thousands of books. Goodness, seemed she was more housekeeper than bookshop owner. She swiped at his artwork with her palm, dislodging dust motes, then wiped them on the leg of her jeans.

After filling him in on her ideas, she waited. His eyes narrowed, and he turned slowly in place, eyeing the shop.

Her breath caught in her throat. Did that mean he liked the concept? Or hated it? She fidgeted, shuffling her feet, stepping on JoJo's tail accidentally. The pup jumped to her feet, yipped, and nuzzled her hand.

"Sorry, girl." Margie dug into her pocket and pulled out a couple of treats. "Sit." After the dog obeyed, she fed her the treats. "I'm spoiling you."

After her foster dog thumped her leg with her killer tail, Margie signaled for her to settle again, and waited for Ed's verdict.

He faced her finally, face straight. Then he smiled, and she relaxed. "I love the idea. I wish somebody had done something like that when I was a kid. I never knew what to read when I went to the library, and I avoided bookstores because they intimidated me with their order and their—their secrets."

"Most bookstore arrange themselves much like a library."

"But they didn't have a helpful librarian sitting behind the desk." His gaze dropped to the floor, and he shuffled a toe on the old hardwood flooring. "Like I said, I was afraid to ask questions." He gestured to the stacks with one hand. "But an event like this simply begs for questions. You could display your books. Securely, of course. And books like them. Same author. Same sub-genre."

She snapped her fingers. "Good idea. I hadn't thought of that." She tilted her head to one side. "Should I take out an ad in the paper?"

He shook his head. "Do people really pay attention? Let your customers know with a flyer in their shopping bags starting this week. Something simple. Email your list. Put up a few signs in the store and the windows. Maybe that sandwich board you used for the spooky Halloween party could get a facelift and draw folks in."

"You're just an idea generator, aren't you?" She paused. "How did you know I needed your help with this?"

He waggled his fingers and hummed the theme song to an old shark movie. "Vulcan mind meld."

She giggled. "You've got your soundtracks mixed up."

"Despite that, you can't argue that I showed up in

the nick of time."

"That you did." She scribbled notes on a sheet of paper she pulled from the drawer beneath the display case. "Anything else?"

"How about that eloping thing?"

"I meant about the store event."

He drew a deep breath, held it for a couple of heartbeats, exhaled, then shook his head. "Nope. Sorry. Exhausted the brain cells on that one."

Margie clicked a couple of buttons and pulled up a document she'd been working on over the past couple of weeks. "Come here and look at this."

He studied the schematics. "That the addition you want to build onto the shop?"

"Yup. Not huge, but it will give me more retail space. And I can move the book binding equipment into the new bit. More windows will make that work go faster."

"Business been picking up?"

"It has. Ever since I updated the website, added in new widgets, orders for restoration and books have poured in from all over the world."

His brow pulled down. "If you don't watch it, you won't have time for me."

She patted his hand. "That will never happen."

Ed's bottom lip jutted out. "I don't know. I've heard of other marriages where one or the other gets so involved in their work, they don't have time for anything else."

This time, she laughed. "Says the police detective with how many open cases?"

"Just cold cases right now. Not quite the same thing. Absolutely not the same urgency."

"But when a homicide comes across your desk, I don't see you for days." She crossed her arms over her chest. "Sometimes I think the only way to get time with you will be to kill somebody."

He laid a finger across her lips. "Don't say that. You know that if I arrest you and haul you off in handcuffs, we'll have to stop dating."

"Like that's going to happen." She pointed to the screen. "I'd like to get this application in to the Planning Department at town hall today. Do you think it's ready?"

"As it will ever be. Print it off. I'll go with you in case those bureaucrats get out of hand."

She clicked on the PRINT button, and the machine in the corner whirred to life, spewing out the pages. Once completed, she stapled the paper together and attached the check she'd written the previous evening.

As they headed out the front door, Margie's cell rang. She glanced at the CALLER ID. "Oh, I want to take this. It's the paving contractor." She handed her key to Ed as she answered. "Hi Carl. It's Margie. Thanks for calling back."

"Been busy."

The man's gruff voice didn't even remotely resemble the cheerful voice mail greeting. In fact, the delay in returning her call and his attitude stopped her in her tracks, and Ed bumped into her from behind. Still, as a friend to her great-aunt, she'd give Mr. Stanley the opportunity to bid on her project. Seemed the right thing to do. "As I said in my message, I'm applying to the town to expand—"

"I know what you're planning."

She held her phone a few inches from her face and glared at it, glad the contractor couldn't see her. How rude. "Well, I wanted to give you—"

"Why don't you build up?"

Not that it was any of his business, but no way would she let his bad manners ruffle her. "As you know, the shop and apartment are already at the limit for the number of stories that the Downtown Planning Committee allows. They won't let me add to the top. Plus, having the store on two levels wouldn't be as convenient for me or for my customers."

"Bet you could get an exception. Ever'body loved Roselda."

"But I'm not her. And I'm not certain this old house could support a third story." What was this man's problem? "Why won't you give me a bid for re-paving my parking lot minus the six or eight spaces the addition will take up?"

"Don't recommend it."

She didn't recall asking if he thought her plan a good idea. "Do you want the business or not?"

"Nope. Too busy."

"Can you suggest another company—"

Silence greeted her. She checked the screen. CALL ENDED.

Beyond rude.

This bordered on the psychotic.

{*}

Ten minutes later, Margie gritted her teeth. She hated waiting. Despised lines. Saw no purpose in delays.

Apparently, the general contractor with a hundred and twelve projects and twice that many questions ahead of her didn't know that about her. If he had, maybe he'd have waited the three and a half minutes it would have taken her to get her business concluded before he arrived.

Ed smiled at her. "Breathe deep. You can do this."

"Dealing with government at any level makes me nervous. Oh, I should have mailed this in. Done it online. Checked my mental health at the door."

He looped his arm through hers. "I'll take you out for coffee. Or ice cream. Or lunch. All three, even. As soon as we're done here."

She groaned. "You might owe me dinner by that time."

"I hope not. I have to get back to work this afternoon."

"See? Already looking for reasons to abandon me here in these hallowed halls of bureaucracy."

He tugged her closer. "Am not. Just sayin', that's all."

The current customer shuffled papers into a file

folder. "Thanks, Nell, for answering all my questions." The man, obviously sensing another opportunity to delay her access to three of her favorite food groups, dropped a paper on the floor. Bending awkwardly from the waist, knees locked in place, he grunted as he stretched his fingers to grip the errant sheet before straightening. He tossed her an awkward grin. "Sorry to keep you waiting. Tryin' to straighten up my parents' estate."

Margie gulped and smiled. As in both mother and father? He was seventy, if he was a day. "No worries."

He nodded to Nell behind the counter. "See you for supper on Saturday."

At this rate, Margie might well join them. Perhaps she should have packed a lunch. Then again, older folks were among her favorite people. Like Grandma Carly, for example. Around the same vintage as this man. And still vital and young in mind, if not in body. Lord willing, she'd be that age herself, some day.

The clerk beckoned to her. "Next?"

Margie explained the purpose of her visit, then shoved her papers across the counter and under the glass partition. "How long does it usually take to get approval?"

Nell clicked her tongue as she scanned the documents. Was that good news? Or bad? "Depends."

"On?"

The woman paused and locked eyes with her. "The head of the planning committee is a stickler for details." She flipped another page and planted a be-ringed forefinger on question twelve. "Take this, for instance."

Margie craned her neck, trying to read upside down. "Parking spaces?"

"Yes. Says here you plan to remove parking spots, yet you also plan to increase retail space."

Her point? "Yes."

"Might seem to Earl Cramer—he's the man making the decisions, mind you—that you can't cut it both ways. Won't more retail space mean more customers?"

Margie chuckled. "That's the idea. But most of my customers walk, or they park along main street, so it shouldn't be a problem. Plus, even with the decrease in parking spaces, there will still be room for about fifty cars."

"Is the lot marked private?"

"No." Margie gulped. Seemed Nell was more persnickety than her boss. "Should it be?"

"If you want the town to consider that all fifty spots belong solely to your business, it needs to be clearly marked. That way, you can tow folks who aren't customers. And Earl—Mr. Cramer—will be more likely to approve."

Was that a tinge of a blush on the woman's cheeks? Something going on between her and the head of the planning committee, perhaps? A factoid Margie would keep to herself. For now.

She pasted on a smile, even though she wanted to reach through the six inches between the counter and the glass and shake the woman. "I'll make sure to post that the parking is for customers of the store."

"Which means you'll need a contract with a towing company."

Margie pulled out her phone and opened her notepad app. "Right. Signs. Towing company." She pressed SAVE, then grinned at Nell. "Good as done. Can we make a note on the relevant sections?"

The clerk's eyes narrowed and her lips pursed. "I don't know. How can I be certain you'll do what you say?"

Ed stepped forward, his arm brushing against Margie's. "Hi, Nell."

"Detective Hogan. What a pleasure." Her glance went from Margie to the handsome officer. "You know each other?"

"We do. We're *very* good friends." He winked. "I'll follow up with Miss Hanson. Keep her in line."

Margie bristled at his words. He'd not shown this side of him before—or was it merely an act to help her through this process? She determined to bring it up. Later. Once she got out in the regular world again.

She patted his arm and giggled. Giggled, her? Really? Whatever it took to get her plans approved. So long as it wasn't illegal or immoral, that is. After all, she had standards. "Detective Hogan thinks I'm a full-time job."

Her Grampa Mike's face filled her mind. That's how he referred to her grandmother, too. Oh, dear. Were she and Ed becoming them?

Nell glanced at her, eyeing her up and down. "I imagine so." She pulled the application close. "I'll make a couple of notes, initial them, and then have you do the same." She glanced up over her eyeglasses. "And I'll mention that Detective Hogan is a personal friend. As a reference only, you understand. He carries a lot of weight in this community."

Margie bit back a groan. Was this small town, nestled in the outskirts of Denver, Colorado, much like Bear Cove, Maine? How long would she live here before natives would consider her trustworthy? She'd heard Grandma Carly make comments about never really fitting in, not being a real resident, even after living and working in Bear Cove for more than twenty years.

Still, if having Ed as an unofficial sponsor sped up the process... "How long should it take to get this approved?"

Nell glanced at the calendar on the wall beside her. "Next committee meeting is Monday."

"Not before then?"

A brisk shake of the head. "Not a chance. He's nose deep in preparing for the launch of Christmas this Saturday."

The pronouncement and tone indicated that the season would risk somebody's wrath should it consider commencing other than in five days' time.

Her heart sank into her shoes like a rock in a pond. Plans to begin construction before Christmas slipped away like a vapor. Then again... "Do you think if

I introduced myself to Mr. Cramer on Saturday, that might speed things up?"

"Perhaps. Couldn't hurt."

Margie turned to Ed. "Do you know Mr. Cramer?"

"Never met the man."

She faced Nell. "Can you describe him?"

Again, that hint of coloring highlighted the clerk's cheeks. "Well, he's tall. Taller than me, anyway. Has lovely blue eyes. His hair is a little thin, but you know what they say."

No, she didn't.

When Margie remained silent, Nell pushed on. "God created some perfect heads, and on the rest, He put hair."

Ed chuckled. "Good one, Nell."

Margie forced a half-smile. "Thank you for your help." She quirked her chin at her fiancé. "Shall we go? I think you owe me lunch. And coffee. And ice cream."

"I'm in."

When they neared the door, he stepped aside to allow her to precede him. She paused and leaned closer. "I'll be nice to this Cramer guy, but here's one thing I know for certain. No low-level bureaucrat will stop my plans."

Chapter 2

The week passed quickly—perhaps too fast. By the end of day on Saturday, Margie collapsed onto her sofa, ready for some downtime. A quiet evening at home might be exactly what the doctor called for. If she needed a medical opinion, that is. Which she didn't.

What she really wanted was a hearty dinner and a great chick flick—she pulled out her cell and checked her schedule.

And groaned. Seemed she'd done a lot of that this past week, beginning with her planning application on Monday. And her call to a couple of local towing companies as she sought to set up an account. Obtaining signage for her parking lot depended on said contract. But every company so far said they were too busy to take on a customer who might call in their services once a month. Or less.

Well, she'd best make a couple of calls before everybody closed for the weekend. She couldn't in good conscience permit Mr. Cramer to believe she'd kept her word if she hadn't.

She dialed the next-to-last tow-er on her list.

A man answered on the second ring. "E-Z Rider Towing. What kin I do fer ya?"

Great. Another example of a hillbilly transplant in the Rockies. She drew a breath. "I need a company to list on my parking lot signage. Are you taking on new accounts?"

"Sure can. Hold on." Rustling paper met her ear, then a loud *thunk!* before the man returned. "Sorry 'bout that. What's your name?"

This was different. "Don't you need to know how many times I might call for service?"

"Nope. Just need the name and address. We charge the owner when they come to get their vehicle." More rustling. "Pencil poised."

She gave him the name of her shop and the street address. "How long will it take to set up the account?"

"Done. And I'll drop off signs on Monday."

"Wait. You provide the notices that the lot belongs to my shop?"

"Sher do. How many?"

"Spaces?"

"Signs do you need?"

"I don't know. There will be about fifty spaces."

"Here's what I'll do. How many access points?"

"Two."

"Gotcha. A double on the post signs. And since your business name is so long, I'll just use BOOKSTORE PARKING ONLY. How does that sound?"

"Perfect."

"Great. See you by end of the day Monday."

Margie stared at her phone after the call disconnected. Wow, that was easy. Everybody else made the process sound so difficult. She set the device down and leaned back against the cushion. If only the rest of her life moved along so smoothly. She closed her eyes. Just for a minute.

When her cell pinged not ten seconds later, she dragged open her eyes. Shadows invaded the living room. A glance toward the window confirmed the sun was but history for today.

She peered at the phone. Ed. *See you in fifteen minutes.*

What the—? Another chime. *Excited to share the Christmas lights tour with you.*

Oh, right. A date with a purpose. Following an opening ceremony of sorts by the mayor, folks followed a walking tour of the biggest displays of lights at about a dozen homes in the town.

Her stomach rumbled, and she dashed to the kitchen for a banana and yogurt, then a quick trip to the bathroom to brush both her teeth and her hair. After checking the forecast and outside temperature on her phone, she donned a Christmas sweater, along with her winter coat, earmuffs, and gloves, took JoJo out for a brisk double circuit of the shop until the pup finally settled and did her business, then straight upstairs again.

She dumped kibble into JoJo's bowl, petting the dog's head as the Lab scarfed down her supper. "You're eating better than me tonight. No worries. I can probably talk Ed into buying a couple of street tacos. Or hotdogs."

Her stomach growled. Was that in agreement? Or warning her about eating from street vendors?

23

A final scratch behind JoJo's ears, and she was ready. Not a moment too early.

True to his word, Ed pulled up in his SUV as she pushed open the door leading to the parking lot. He exited and came around, holding open the passenger door for her.

She smiled up at him, apparently providing the perfect target for his lips on hers. Which she didn't mind. Tingles ran down her spine, all the way to her toes. Making her want more.

He experienced the same reaction, judging by the way he moaned when he stepped away. "I hope you don't want a long engagement."

She giggled. "You're the one who wants to wait until the party to make it official." When she sat, he leaned in, his aftershave—spicy and outdoorsy—tickling her nose. "I'd marry you tomorrow in the courthouse."

He straightened. "No way. And have your family hate me for the rest of my life?"

She waited until he resumed the driver's seat and turned the car around to enter the street. "They wouldn't hate you that long. Just for about twenty years."

He shivered. "And your Grandma Carly? She'd give me the evil eye. I don't stand a chance with her."

Margie giggled. "She can seem quite ferocious, but she's really a softy underneath."

"Must be deep as the Grand Canyon. No. We'll wait to get married until after Christmas at least so we don't mess up their holiday plans."

She peered at him. "Are you having cold feet already?"

"Nope." He made the turn toward town hall and pulled into a spot in the lot. "Well, maybe a tinge of frostbite."

Her breath caught in her throat, and she glanced at her left hand. Where her engagement ring had rested for all of about two hours when he first asked her to marry him. Her right hand touched the base of her neck. Yep, there it was. "Really?"

He faced her, grinning. "No."

She mock-punched his arm, which he gripped, then howled as though she'd grievously wounded him. "Don't scare me like that."

His eyes widened as he rubbed his bicep. "I've learned my lesson. Believe me."

She shook her head and waited for him to open her door. Not that she needed that courtesy. But he enjoyed treating her like a lady. And honestly, she appreciated his attentions and his good manners.

They crossed the parking lot hand in hand and rounded the building to the courtyard area, now filled with hundreds of citizens of all ages. Babes in snuggly packs, toddlers in strollers, and even a few in harnesses as parents struggled to maintain control of their kiddoes. Pressed in from all sides, Margie lost hold of Ed, who rapidly disappeared from sight ahead of her. Funny how her hand chilled instantly in his absence.

Once gathered around the tree, she spotted him

25

across the circle of faces. He held up one finger, then ducked back into the crowd. Within a couple of minutes, he appeared at her elbow.

Jostled from behind, he slipped his arm through hers and tugged her close. "Not letting go this time."

She smiled. "Good thing we didn't hold on, or my fingers would drag on the ground by now."

He nodded and snuggled against her. "Is it my imagination, or is it warmer on this side?"

"Must be your wild imaginings, sir."

The mayor exited the town hall and approached the microphone on the makeshift platform. Once the crowd quieted, she stepped up and delivered her greetings on behalf of the council and employees. "I know it's a little chilly out here tonight." She paused as the crowd laughed. "And I know the wee ones will soon want their beds."

An old-timer added his thoughts. "And us bigger wee ones, too, Mayor Young."

A round of applause accompanied his comment, and Madam Mayor waited until the crowd silenced. "I declare the Edgewater Christmas Lights tour officially open." Loud cheers. "Select your path according to your own preferences. We have three-block, six-block, and ten-block tours. Regardless of which you choose, plan to stop in at the retailers along the way. Hopefully, you brought an appetite, too, as we have local street vendors stationed to keep your energy up. Not to mention that at the town park, you can boost your spirits in the beer and wine tent, and, as always, there is plenty of free hot chocolate and snacks at our very own North Pole. We'll light the tree promptly at eight-thirty, then you are all welcome to stay on for as long as you want. Happy holidays!"

Margie gripped Ed's hand as the crowd stepped forward. By the time they'd gone half a block, however, the surrounding numbers had thinned considerably. She tapped the map he held. "Seems most are heading directly for hot drinks and food."

He leaned toward her. "Is that what you'd like to do?"

"Well, the yogurt and banana I had earlier didn't last long."

"Your wish is my command." He pointed. "We can go along here, then turn at the second left. Town Park is only three blocks from there."

They oohed and aahed over the light shows and inflatable characters at the next mini-mansion. LED snowflakes covered the naked boughs of the aspen and ash at the second home, and a life-size manger scene filled the yard of the third.

Margie gripped the fence and studied the figures. "It's so real, I expect Mary to look up at me."

Ed nodded. "Sometimes the pages of scripture seem so sanitized when we read the story. The familiar words don't capture the reality of the situation."

Her eyes watered. The wind, perhaps? Or the scene before her. Having grown up in a Bible-believing family, her father read the story every Christmas morning.

27

She practically knew the verses by heart. So why did this simple manger, complete with plastic figures in a yard strewn with hay in Colorado, touch her so much? Because she was away from family for the first time in her life over this special season? Because she was preparing to step into a new role as wife? Or something else?

She sniffled, then dug into her pocket for a tissue, swiping at her frozen nose. "Let's go."

Ed peered at her. "You okay?"

"A little cold."

He gripped her hand and tucked it inside his jacket pocket. She relished the warmth, the strength, and the image of unity. Protected by love.

What a perfect picture.

Picking up their pace, they covered the three blocks to the park in short order, their breath floating off on the chill night air. An even larger group waited at the tree. Margie glanced at her cell. Four minutes early. Not bad.

Three minutes later, Mayor Young clambered up on the stage, followed by a boy and a girl scout. Once again, the crowd edged forward, despite the amplified sound system and the sixty-foot tree.

And once again, Margie lost her grip on Ed's hand.

She exhaled, scanning the crowd for him. Standing on tip-toes, she struggled to maintain her balance. Another sigh. At this rate, she wouldn't find him until next Christmas.

Pressure from behind to move forced her to choose. The corner of the stage neared, now less than ten feet away. Last time, he'd ended up across from her. Maybe if she went around the rear of the structure, she'd find him.

Excusing herself at least a hundred times, she veered off in that direction, intent on getting back to where there should be fewer people. The mayor's voice thundered from the speakers within arm's reach, and Margie ducked lower to avoid the blast on her ears. The crowd cheered and applauded. Something about the scouts plugging in the lights. Or throwing the switch. She wasn't quite certain.

Around the back corner of the wooden stage, she paused and leaned against the wall, catching her breath. Much quieter here. She could almost hear her heart pounding from the exertion. More applause, and the tree lights cast a prism-like hue on the area behind the stage. Cheers. A small choir struck up a Christmas hymn. *O Little Town of Bethlehem.*

Nice. One of her favorites.

A loud bang.

Oh, dear. Was the little drummer boy not getting enough attention?

She glanced around. That wasn't a drumbeat.

Or a car backfire, as her brain scrambled to hope, then discard the thought.

Sounded more like fireworks. But who'd fire off just the one cracker?

29

Or a gunshot.

Footsteps ran in the opposite direction, and she pushed away from the wall. A bundle of carpet—or something—lay flat in the snow less than twenty feet away. Swallowing back the lump in her throat, she trotted in that direction.

As she neared, details became more apparent in the diffused light. Not carpet. A body. She made out the booted feet. Pants. Jacket.

Assuming the name on the coat proved correct, Earl Cramer lay on his back, staring up at the eternity of space.

With a bullet hole in his forehead.

She knelt, something hard beneath her knee. She scooted aside. This was no time to injure herself with a buried rock. Shoving her gloved hand into the snow, she lifted the object.

A handgun.

Get rid of the gun. It's likely the murder weapon. Her logical brain rebuked her for picking it up in the first place. Isn't that how folks got themselves arrested on murder shows on television?

At the scene of the crime, holding the murder weapon.

{*}

Ed rounded the building, patting his right hip where his service revolver usually sat. But not tonight. Off-duty, he'd thought, as he prepared for the evening with his best girl. No need to conceal carry. Who would cause trouble

30

requiring him to carry a sidearm at a Christmas tree lighting?

Well, somebody hadn't gotten the memo about peace and joy to all mankind.

He waved off the three officers close on his heels. "Keep the crowd back. Get a list of everybody here in case we need to ask questions. Confiscate all cell phones and cameras until we see if they caught anything in photos or video."

The trio veered off and returned to the front of the venue, while Ed slowed, hugging the rear wall of the stage. If the perpetrator was still here, they might wait for first responders.

His breath, ragged from adrenaline and the cold, threatened to rip holes in his lungs. Caution urged him to slow, while expediency pressed him on. Somebody could be hurt. Maybe kids fooling around with fireworks. No. He shook his head. He knew the difference. That was definitely a gunshot. Handgun, he suspected. Didn't have the deep growl of a shotgun, or the high-pitched *thwap*! of a rifle.

And where was Margie? After losing contact with her—again—he'd spent the past minutes searching the crowd. Maybe they needed to avoid large gatherings.

Ahead, something on the ground. And somebody beside that something. The tree lights, now flashing spasmodically in time with a silent melody, glinted off metal.

Once again, he wished he'd been more prudent.

No weapon. No taser. Not even pepper spray. Maybe he could trick them into thinking he was armed.

"Stop. Police." He pointed his hand in imitation of a gun. "Down on the ground."

The item in their hand dropped, and the person sprawled, face down, in the snow, in a poor imitation of a snow angel. He stepped closer and planted his foot in the middle of their back before looking at what he now knew was a body. The head of the planning committee. Dead.

The person under his foot shifted, turning their face toward him. "Ed?"

Margie? Dear God, no. "What are you doing here?"

"I heard the shot. I was looking for you."

A constable appeared from the opposite direction. "Detective, we—" His eyes widened. "Got him already? Good on you."

Ed's heart sank. Yes, he'd caught his man. Or should he say, his woman?

His fiancée, actually.

Could things get any worse?

Chapter 3

"Oh, God, I'm scared."

Margie sat on the hard wooden bench in the lobby of the Edgewater Police Department. The metal cuffs on her wrists pinched, despite Ed's assurances he had them on as loose as he could. She exhaled. What a predicament she'd put them both in. She brought in for questioning about the death of a man she'd never even met. And he unable to use his influence to spare her.

Although he'd spent the entirety of the three-minute trip from the town park to the police station assuring her he didn't believe her responsible for Earl Cramer's death. Well, he'd say that, wouldn't he, even if he did? Get her to let her guard down. Confess right away. Clear up an open case before breakfast.

A detective's dream.

Well, her nightmare. A horror story and a bad dream rolled into one.

If that was true, she should wake up soon, safe and sound in her bed.

Margie dug a fingernail into the back of her hand. Ow, that hurt. Not asleep, then.

She looked up at the sound of footsteps. Ed. She stood. "Oh, I'm so glad it's you."

He gestured for her to sit. "I can't take the lead on

this." He peered into her eyes. "You understand, don't you?"

"Come on, Ed. You know I didn't do this. I couldn't."

"I know, but—"

The front door burst open, and a familiar face stepped through. Nell, from the planning department.

Margie stiffened. Based on the grimace on the woman's face, this wasn't good.

Nell pointed at her, stabbing the air with her finger and her words. "That's her. She's the one who said she wouldn't let Mr. Cramer stop her. No matter what."

Margie half-rose, but Ed pushed her back to the bench. "That's not what I said."

The clerk rushed toward her, and Ed stepped between the two. Nell thrashed, working to escape his grip. "She did. She said she'd do whatever it took to get her way." She sniffed, cheeks red. "You haven't lived here but a heartbeat. And now you've murdered the best thing this town ever had."

Ed directed Nell toward the desk sergeant. "Please look after her. Get her a cup of coffee. Find somebody to take her statement."

Margie shook her head. "She's lying. You were there, Ed. I didn't say—"

"Don't say anything else until your attorney comes."

She stared at him. The man she planned to spend the rest of her life with. The man whose ring she wore on a chain. Would wear on her finger except for his desire to make a big deal of the engagement. "My attorney? You haven't read me my rights." She rattled the cuffs in his face. "Although I should have figured out this wasn't the simple friendly conversation you said, shouldn't I?"

His warm hands pressed against hers, and she lowered her hands and sat again. She forced a smile. "So who's going to interrogate me? Should I expect a rubber hose? Water torture?"

He rubbed her back, his hand strong even through all her layers. "We don't use rubber hoses anymore." He tossed her a half-smile that failed to ease the worry lines around his eyes. "Commander Morgan. He's fair. He'll listen."

"I'm in trouble, aren't I?"

"I'd say so, yes."

"And you can't help me, can you?"

"I need to distance myself from the investigation. Not allowed anywhere near evidence. And we can't talk about the case."

"Should I call my parents?"

He glanced at the Regulator clock, its black frame in stark contrast to its white face and the pale green walls. Whoever said green was calming never lived on the ocean. All she saw when she stared at the chipped paint were angry breakers in a nor'easter.

"It's what—three hours earlier there, right? Five o'clock. Let them sleep. We'll know more soon."

She nodded. Was that a promise?

35

Or a threat?

{*}

Ed crossed his arms over his chest and watched through the two-way mirror as the commander strode into the interview room and introduced himself.

His superior nodded to the female police officer standing quietly in the corner. "You can remove the cuffs."

Once the constable did, Margie sat back in the plastic chair, hands in her lap. "Thank you. Ed— Detective Hogan said you were fair."

"I like to think I am."

Morgan tossed a thin file folder on the table, then sat opposite her. That was a good sign, wasn't it? Not much evidence against her. Then again, he hadn't given his statement yet. And Nell's likely wasn't typed up, either.

Margie's shoulders slumped a fraction of an inch. Ed understood completely. Exhausted. Frightened. Hungry. Alone. Did she think he'd abandoned her? Turned his back when she most needed him? He offered a quick prayer for God the sustainer to accompany her.

Commander Morgan tapped the file. "You are not under arrest."

"Yet."

He blinked twice then his mouth lifted. "You are probably wondering what happens next."

"Yes."

"First, I hear you out. Ask a few questions. Then

36

we go from there."

She settled, pressing her shoulder blades into the chair. "Fair enough."

"So, tell me what happened."

She filled the commander in on her journey around the stage, neglecting to mention she'd attended the event with an Edgewater police detective. Heard the noise. Thought it was fireworks. Saw the body. Knew it was Cramer because of the name embroidered on the jacket.

When she finished, she exhaled. "That's it, I guess."

"So you'd never met?"

Margie locked eyes with the man. "Never. Nell at town hall gave me a brief description, but as I'm sure you noticed, she has a crush on him."

A tiny smile appeared, easing the taut lines around the commander's mouth. "I had noticed."

She leaned forward, hands on the table. "So she's not exactly an unbiased witness, is she?"

"Did you say you wouldn't let Cramer get in your way?"

"I didn't mention him by name."

Ed nodded, although he stood alone in the observation room. She spoke truth. Not that he expected anything less from her. From the woman he planned to marry.

"Did you see him at the tree lighting before you found his body?"

"Not that I'm aware of. But then again, I wasn't looking for him. And until I saw his name on his jacket, I didn't know for certain it was him."

A knock drew the attention of all three. A uniformed officer stepped in, set a sheet of paper on the table, and withdrew. The lock clicked back into place from the outside, loud, or so it seemed to Ed. Echoing off the walls. And he wasn't even the one being questioned.

Commander Morgan glanced at the report. "Says here they found GSR on your gloves."

Gunshot residue. Could be evidence she'd fired the weapon.

"Of course. I picked up the weapon. In my left hand."

Ed resisted smacking his forehead. An excellent piece of rebuttal recollection there.

"I'm right-handed. Unlikely I'd have worn my gloves on the wrong hands, is it? And had the foresight to switch them back?"

"If it was premeditated, you might." Morgan shifted in his seat. The man was an exceptional interrogator, but that was a tell that confirmed he struggled with the evidence. "Criminals have to be smart to avoid getting arrested."

"But I'm not a criminal. And if I wanted to get away, I could have run." She leaned back in her chair. "Whose gun was it?"

"Huh?"

"I don't own one. Did Cramer? Did he come to a tree lighting event packing a weapon? If so, maybe he was worried about somebody."

"It was his weapon. Duly registered. With a CHP license."

Concealed handgun permit.

Her head tilted to one side. "Is that a concealed carry?"

"It is. You've picked up the lingo quick, considering you've been here about a year."

"A little more, actually. I'm a quick study."

Careful, Margie. Don't come off as knowing too much or mocking him.

Morgan stood. "We're charging you with involuntary manslaughter, given it wasn't your weapon. Footprint evidence leads us to believe you encountered him, you scuffled, he pulled the gun, and it went off. First offense, ties to the community. Bond will be ten thou and agreeing to report for court. Can you make it?"

"I don't have that kind of cash available, but I have several valuable manuscripts I can put up for collateral. Will that suffice?"

He nodded. "Follow me, and I'll have Officer Payton here take you to the booking room for formalities. She'll call a bondsman to arrange for your release."

Margie faced the mirror and gave him a half smile. Although he longed to hold her in his arms and tell her everything would be all right, Ed turned from the window. Wishing the clock would turn back and everybody could have a do-over wouldn't make it happen.

Margie was in a barrel load of trouble.

And there was little he could do to help.

Chapter 4

When her alarm sounded on Sunday morning, Margie rolled over in bed and groaned. JoJo, however, communicated in no uncertain terms what she expected: a walk, breakfast, and maybe another jaunt later on. Or two.

The fact her owner had less than three hours of sleep meant nothing to the canine.

After a very cold and wet nose nudged under the blankets for the third time, Margie gave in. "You're right. I have to get up. At least I didn't spend the entire night in the hoosegow."

She flung off the covers, determined to begin this day better than it deserved. Then again, being Sunday, the Lord's Day, He should receive her very best.

"God, forgive my attitude. You hold every one of my days in Your hand." She shivered when her feet touched the bare floor. Had He also held Cramer's life? She certainly hoped so. "And God, be with his family, please, at this difficult time. Amen."

Armed with the power of prayer, she now felt more equipped to face the day.

Whatever it brought.

She moved through the next couple of hours in automatic mode, her mind still fixed on the previous night's events. What started so innocently then became so traumatic. Trying to place herself in the shoes of others only muddled her brain even more: next of kin when the police came to their door to tell them their loved one wasn't coming home. Ever again. Ed. Was there even a tiny little spot of him that wondered if she might have done this? Even unintentionally?

And if the situation were reversed, would she honestly wonder if he was capable of such an action?

After walking the dog, dropping more kibbles into her bowl, making coffee and eating a bowl of cereal that still rumbled around her tummy, she decided a hot shower was in order, certain she still smelled like jail. JoJo sat in the middle of the bathroom floor and waited, panting and tongue lolling when Margie stepped out after draining the hot water supply.

She smiled at the pup. "You always think I'm going to disappear in here, don't you?"

Maybe today would be a good one to step through a magical doorway into another world where she wasn't a suspect in a murder.

She dried off, and although her skin was pink with heat, her insides still trembled. She flipped on the switch for the heat lamp as she dried her hair and put on a little makeup to cover the pallor from her prison ordeal.

As she brushed on mascara, she chuckled. She'd been in custody, not even jail.

And if she didn't figure out who killed Earl Cramer, she'd be spending much more time in the big house.

Imagine her complexion then. No. Too horrible

to even contemplate. She'd figure this out.

Or die trying.

She clapped a hand over her mouth.

Best keep those thoughts to herself.

{*}

From the sidewalk outside the main entrance of the church, Ed scanned the parking lot, looking for Margie's car. At ten minutes before service time, she pulled in, parked, and got out. He waved and trotted over to meet her, planting a chaste kiss on her pale cheek.

Then he held her at arm's length and peered into her eyes. "Did you get any sleep?"

Her fingers brushed her face. "Do I look that bad?"

"No, you're beautiful, as always."

She gripped his jacket sleeve. "I'm so sorry for all the trouble I'm causing."

He hugged her, rubbing her back, and speaking into her ear. "It's not your fault. We'll get through this." The church bells chimed, alerting them that service would start in two minutes. He gripped her hand. "Come on. Don't want to be late."

They nodded to several almost-late arrivals. He studied each one's expression but detected no change of attitude toward either him or Margie. Appeared nobody took the time to read their paper this morning. Or perhaps the news broke too late and wouldn't print until later in the day.

He prayed something bigger and more important

overrode the story, but except for catastrophe or political intrigue, that was unlikely.

Next Sunday might be interesting. Once word gets out. Unless we've tracked the real killer by then and Margie's been cleared.

He led Margie to their usual section, front right, and they slid into two chairs as the pastor stepped onto the platform. After introducing himself and welcoming everybody, he opened the service with prayer, then asked them to stand and worship.

Ed pushed all thoughts of work and trouble from his mind, entering the Lord's presence wholeheartedly. For the two worship songs at the conclusion of the music, he held Margie's hand. Her fingers, cold to the touch, gripped his like a lifeline. A couple of times he glanced over at her, but wet eyes and a trembling bottom lip assured him she wasn't as okay as she wanted him to believe.

The pastor resumed the platform and introduced the sermon, "Nothing is Easy". Ed grunted. Had the pastor learned of the previous night's events? Did the man's eyes seek them out? Fix on them as though preaching only to him? To Margie?

Ed heaved a sigh when the pastor's focus shifted to another section of the congregation. Of course he wasn't speaking only to them. That would be wrong, wouldn't it? Yet the topic was timely. About how the early apostles and followers faced many struggles as they tried to live out their faith in a world that hated them. And, fast-forwarding two thousand years, how today's believers can expect the same.

Well, that explained a lot about his and Margie's current circumstances. Although how her faith brought on this horrendous charge against her was beyond his understanding. Did God have something up His sleeve? Or was the enemy of their souls working overtime to bring her down? Or was it him the devil sought?

While he found comfort in knowing he wasn't alone in his walk, he had plenty of questions by the time the sermon ended.

He turned to Margie. "Are you still on for lunch?"

She nodded. "I'd like that. If it's okay. I don't want you to get in trouble."

"Trouble?"

"Fraternizing with the criminal element." She giggled. "Never thought I'd refer to myself that way."

He nodded to a couple stepping past them to exit their row, leaned closer and lowered his voice. "Under the law, you aren't a criminal until proven guilty."

"Really." She glanced around. "Then why do I feel like I've already been convicted?"

"Not by anybody here." He tapped his chest. "Including me."

"Really?" Her eyes watered again, causing the lump in his throat to grow by at least fifty percent. "Honestly? You wouldn't lie to me?"

"Never."

{*}

After settling into the booth at the 5810 Diner, Margie shrugged out of her coat and settled in as Ed smiled across the table at her.

The server appeared at their table, placing ice water and a menu before each of them, then disappeared to deal with another table where a toddler tipped his entire plate of mac and cheese into his lap and now howled like a banshee.

Margie smiled toward the embarrassed parents and flustered server. "Life could be worse, I guess."

Ed nodded. "Sure could." He tapped the plastic-covered food offering list. "The regular?"

"I believe so. Comfort food."

"Great. Two liver and onions it is then."

The young girl waiting tables reappeared, cheeks flushed. "Sorry. Had to clean up—" She giggled. "You know."

Margie did. She had a younger brother, and at that age, he'd been clumsy, too. Particularly with things that made a mess. Mac and cheese, milk, soda, mustard. She glanced at the girl's nametag. "Molly, I think we're ready to order."

She named her plate, chose tea instead of coffee or soda, then sat back as Ed placed his me-too request. When Molly turned to leave, Margie caught her attention.

"We pray and thank God for our food. Is there anything we could pray for you about?"

Molly stared at her a moment, then her eyes filled with tears. "Thank you. My younger brother is mixed up

46

with some shady folks, and I'm worried about him. His name is Jesse."

Margie patted her hand. "I'm sorry to hear that. And we'll definitely pray." She nodded toward Ed. "He's a police officer. I'm sure he'd be happy to help if he can."

Molly snatched her hand away as if burned. "He doesn't live around here. Lives in—lives in—in Kansas."

Unlikely, but the girl sure didn't want the cops to know where her brother really resided.

Ed's eyebrows raised and lowered. "Sure made her nervous."

The doors into the kitchen swung lazily on their hinges. "Can't think why."

Ed snorted. "Let's pray. Particularly that our food arrives safely and on time." He bowed his head and led them in a short but sincere prayer, including a petition for Jesse and his sister. Once done, he released Margie's hand and studied her. "Is it my imagination, or are you more beautiful with every day?"

She chuckled. "Must be love." She pulled a notebook from her purse. "Speaking of which, the engagement party is a week from tomorrow. We should talk through the details."

"I was thinking finger foods, non-alcoholic beverages, instrumental music in the background, paper plates. and plastic cups. For about twenty people."

"Sounds good to me. Except that's just your guest list, right?"

He blinked. "No, in total."

"But I run a business, and I should invite my customers. Particularly the loyal ones. Not to mention my bookseller, vendors, and the folks who operate businesses in my area."

He exhaled. "Whoo-hoo." His shoulders rose and fell. "Fine with me."

"Two hours should do it, I think. We don't want to feed people for longer than that."

"True."

She jotted several notes on her list, then looked up. "I'll plan for fifty, and if we run out of food and drink, we run out."

Margie glanced at the table where the toddler and his parents sat. The wife's gaze met hers then jerked away. The woman whispered something to her husband, who then turned and glanced at Margie. *Strange.*

But stranger still was that almost every diner exhibited the same bizarre behavior. Whispers. Pointing. Averted gazes. One patron called to Molly, who scribbled out their bill and handed it to him. He and the man with him strode to the register and paid, scurrying out the door in less than thirty seconds.

Like the plague—or something—had descended on the restaurant. Margie inhaled, then breathed out slowly.

She turned to Ed. "Did you notice those two men acting bizarrely?"

"Nope." He sipped his water. "Like how?"

"They practically ran out."

"Did they pay their bill?"

"Well, yes."

"Maybe they remembered somewhere they needed to be."

Could be. But she doubted it.

Molly appeared through the door from the kitchen with two plates in her hands, which she thunked on the table, then pivoted on her heel without a word.

How rude. "She didn't even ask if we needed anything."

"Well, we don't. Let's dig in while it's hot."

Despite concerns about her fellow diners, Margie discovered after the first bite that she was hungry, and soon both plates were empty except for a few smears of gravy. Ed paid the bill and led the way to the car.

After settling her in the car, he leaned close. "Want to walk the dogs around Sloane's Lake?"

"Sounds like a great idea."

Within twenty minutes, he parked in the south lot, and they exited with their guide dogs in training. Bruno, Ed's German shepherd, bounced on the end of his leash, grabbing the length and shaking it like a rag doll. JoJo sat demurely, her hunting dog nose sniffing the air.

The foursome set off, and Margie breathed deep to relieve the knot at the base of her neck. They'd not walked far enough to warm up, however, and she found herself laughing at the antics of her companions—two-legged and four-legged.

"Seriously, you guys, I don't know which of you is

the most childlike."

Both dogs barked their vote, jumping up with snowy paws and planting them on Ed's jacket.

She laughed. "It's unanimous!"

A snowball soared dangerously close to her ear, and she ducked. "No fair! You didn't give me any warning."

He laughed and stepped behind a tree, all wide-eyed and innocent. "Are you accusing me of throwing something?"

A brief battle of misshapen blobs of wet snow occurred, with the dogs tangling themselves around their legs until she and Ed collapsed into the snow alongside the path, breathless. After a few minutes, she sat up and unwound the leashes while Ed submitted to the pups' face-washing with their rough tongues.

Once they were on their way again, Margie asked a question foremost on her mind. "Does Commander Morgan have any other suspects on his list for Cramer's killing?"

"I couldn't say."

"Has he looked around to see if anybody else had a grudge against the man?"

Ed focused on the path. "Can't say."

"What about——?"

He stopped her by laying his hand on her arm. "We can't discuss an open case. You know that."

"Is that all this is to you? Another case?"

"Of course not. And that's what makes it so

difficult."

Hope seeped away like an icicle on a summer's day. "I suppose if I'm not convicted, that will make you look bad, right? Favoritism and all that?"

"It's why we approach every case the same way. Not only must justice be done, but it must be seen to be done."

She snorted. "Didn't seem very just to me in the diner today. All those people. I hope none of them is on my jury. They'd convict me in a heartbeat. You saw them."

"I did. It's called herd mentality."

She gripped his hands. "But who's to say that there won't be people just like that—"

"We've got to believe that none of this caught God by surprise, right?"

She bit her bottom lip. "Yes."

"Faith that He has this under control, right?"

"Yes."

"And courage to face whatever happens?"

"Uh-huh." She looked up at him, her eyes blurred, his profile smudged by her tears. "You know I'm not guilty, right? No matter what anybody else says? I didn't kill Earl Cramer."

He pulled her close, his mouth near her ear. "I know you didn't. You couldn't. We'll get through this somehow."

That's what worried her the most.

The somehow bit.

Chapter 5

With the evening stretching ahead of her after Ed left, Margie spent time in the book binding area of the shop sorting through storage boxes. Mindless work, sort of. When she inherited the house from Aunt Roselda, boxes occupied every nook and cranny of the non-retail space. Might take her mind off her troubles as she explored and prepared for renovations.

Not to sound cold or callous—okay, maybe a little—somebody would take Cramer's place and approve her application. His death wouldn't stop the slowly grinding gears of bureaucracy.

She worked her way through half a dozen boxes, mostly old volumes requiring repair. Nothing particularly valuable, although once restored to salable condition, would enhance her Vintage Manuscript section. While her truly priceless volumes nestled against velvet in the display case under the register, the Vintage section offered less-pricey copies of books that looked great on a shelf. She had several customers who regularly browsed the corner, hoping against hope to find a great steal.

She set those to be restored aside, tossed out a trash sac of old newspapers, and set out a crate of free magazines dating back to the 1970s. Seemed Aunt

Roselda threw nothing out.

Margie glanced at the clock. The last two hours passed quickly. Well, maybe not so. Her feet ached and her back screamed for a rest.

She scooted the stack of a dozen books to the repair table, then perched on a raised stool with a half-back, pressing against the support. Feet hooked on the rungs, she bent over the project, intent on leaving the room as uncluttered as possible.

When her back screamed for relief by cramping, she straightened and stretched her arms over her head. The small window provided little illumination, particularly this late on a December day, so she crossed the room and flipped on the light. Fluorescent lights flickered, then lit the room. A much tidier space, even if she had to say it herself.

Which, since JoJo slept upstairs and said little except *woof!* meant she must speak her own praises. "You've done a great job, Margie. Your mother would be proud of you."

The mention of her mom brought tears to her eyes. She'd refrained from calling and alerting the family about her situation. Except what was it, exactly? Out on bail. Involuntary manslaughter. How to explain? Surely such a minor story in a town in Colorado wouldn't ever hit the national news. But what if it did? Could she really wait any longer?

She added the now-restored books to her inventory through her POS system, priced and then shelved them. Standing back, she admired her handiwork. Something not quite right. Switching the two on the end with the ones beside made the layout more aesthetically appealing. A swipe to remove the dust from the edge of the shelf, and she was done.

Just in time. She dragged herself up the stairs and into her apartment. JoJo lifted her head and wagged her tail. "Not going out yet, girl. Maybe in an hour. I need something to eat."

The pup knew that word and trotted over to her bowls. Margie spooned canned food into one, dumped dry into the other, and checked the automatic waterer. Three-quarters full. Good for now.

Settling in the living room with a grilled cheese sandwich and a glass of milk, Margie turned on the television. Time for something even more mind-numbing than boxes of books. The local news anchor, a perky blonde, smiled back at her.

"Thanks, Rob, for updating us on that story fresh from Edgewater."

Margie froze mid-chew, her finger still on the remote. Was it possible this town had more than one newsworthy story?

She certainly hoped so.

Melissa continued, smiling through the words. "So that's all we know for now. A local businesswoman, whose identity hasn't been released officially, was found hovering over the body, murder weapon in hand. Apparently, the deceased and the suspect had words

54

earlier on Friday over an application to the planning department."

Not true. She'd not spoken to Cramer. Wasn't hovering. This woman made it sound like she was guilty.

Which she wasn't.

"Witnesses have come forward claiming to have overheard the suspect threaten the victim if he didn't approve a re-zoning application. More news after this commercial break."

Oh, no. Now I'll have to let my family know.

She turned off the television and picked up her cell phone, determined to put a good face on the situation. Smile. That's it. Communicate positivity and hope.

If only.

{*}

Ed strode the hallway leading to Commander Morgan's office in response to an email summons. He sighed. Why had he thought it a good idea to pop into the office and clear a couple of reports from his desk? He should have gone straight home and napped with the dog through college football.

But no. He wanted a jump on a busy week. An hour. That should do it.

The door stood open, but he paused and knocked. "Commander? Ed Hogan."

Morgan sat behind his uncluttered desk. He looked up from the computer screen occupying a quarter of the space and peered at him over his bifocals. "Come in. Close the door and take a seat."

While his superior officer appeared relaxed, the voice shouted authority. For a split second, Ed wondered if anybody ever defied the man. If so, what was his reaction? Well, he wasn't the one to find out. Not while Margie's neck hung in the noose.

After settling in the chair opposite his commander, he folded his hands in his lap. "You emailed."

"I did. Need to talk about the Earl Cramer case."

"Sir."

"We've had another piece of evidence that doesn't bode well for our suspect."

Ed's stomach flip-flopped. Could things get any worse?

"I believe you were present when she submitted the application for renovations to her store?"

"I was, sir."

"Well, we located that application. He denied it."

"Already? Margie was told the committee didn't meet for another week."

The commander shrugged. "I guess he didn't need to take it to them. Maybe a technicality. Don't know. Don't care. Now it's more than circumstantial."

Ed shook his head. "Sir, this makes little sense. I heard her mutter that she wouldn't permit any low-level bureaucrat to stop her, but she didn't mention Cramer by name. Nor did she scream it out as some witnesses allege."

"See, that's the problem, Hogan. You're too close to the situation."

"I'm engaged to the woman, if that's what you mean."

"It's not just that, although, if I were you, I might rethink that part of the relationship."

Ed's mouth went dry, and he took a couple of breaths to work up enough spit to speak. "That's not the words of the man I thought you were, sir. With due respect."

Morgan peered at him then nodded. "I guess you're right. If I was in the same situation, I'd want to believe her, too."

"I don't want to believe she's innocent, sir. I know she is. She couldn't—"

"Everybody is capable of killing another, if pushed hard and far enough. Don't fool yourself that you know anybody—not even yourself—so well as to be absolutely certain of what they could or would do."

"Understood. If this had been a case of self-defense, or protecting another, I'd agree. But Margie Hanson wouldn't kill another person."

"She's charged with involuntary manslaughter. I believe she didn't go there to kill him. But they argued—"

"There is no evidence of that, sir. No witnesses heard even a single word passing between them. She did not know he'd be there."

"She says."

"Well, how could she?"

57

"He's a town employee. Most likely, every worker was present. She could have surmised—"

"But how would she know he'd be there behind the stage? She went there looking for me."

The commander shook his head. "Why would she think you'd be there? At exactly the same moment her archenemy was present?" Another shake. "I find that even more difficult to believe."

"No, sir. We got separated by the flow of the crowd. I ended up on the opposite side from her. Rather than pushing through all those people, she took a shortcut behind the stage."

"I don't think so. I think she went there looking for him. You're lucky she used his weapon. Otherwise, it would be a murder charge."

The words echoed through Ed's brain, not connecting. Not making sense. Margie wouldn't. Couldn't. He knew it. How to convince Morgan?

But when he opened his mouth to respond, the commander raised a hand to stop him. "Enough. You're not on this case. We shouldn't really be having this conversation. This is an open investigation. I've already said too much."

Ed's shoulders slumped. He understood protocol. If suspicions of police interference contaminated the case, Margie might never be free of the charges, at least in the public's eye. And the actual killer might get away scot-free.

He leaned forward, hands clasped on the desk. As

if in supplication. "Are you looking at other suspects?"

"Can't say."

His commander's response mirrored his own to Margie just a few hours before. Had the words irritated her as much as they now did him? "So why did you call me in, if not to discuss the case?"

"To ask you to put distance between you and the suspect."

"She has a name, sir. Margie Hanson."

"Regardless, you must appear unconnected. You aren't part of the investigation, and I won't have you calling our department or the integrity of our officers or the case into question. Do I make myself clear?"

"Does that include phone calls?"

"No contact. Period."

"We're engaged, sir. We're planning to announce formally at a party next Monday. To our friends and the community. How do we do that if we can't be together?"

Morgan exhaled heavily, as though he bore the weight of the world on his shoulders. "You can't. You won't. I'd suggest you put off the announcement until we conclude the investigation. It wouldn't look good on your record that you were engaged to her if she's found guilty. And it will look less than stellar if I place a formal warning on your professional record. You could face suspension or even dismissal if you disobey."

Ed stood, arms straight at his side. "Can I at least call her and let her know what's going on?"

"Nothing about the case. Explain that for both of

you, you can't meet, call, or email until we resolve the case."

Ed nodded and pivoted, leaving the office. Wanting to run. All the way to Margie's house. To gather her into his arms and reassure her he'd not let something simple like a job or a black mark in his record stop them from marrying.

But he wouldn't do that. He'd call and explain, and they wouldn't have contact for as long as it took to clear up this mess.

It didn't take a genius to figure out what the commander was really saying: they had their suspect, and until proven innocent, they had no interest in any other cluttering up their case. After all, juries didn't take seriously a case where more than one suspect was charged with a crime. Undermined the whole *beyond a reasonable doubt* thing.

No, if Margie was to be released from these charges, then he had to do the one thing Commander Morgan warned him—in an obtuse way—not to do.

Find the actual killer.

{*}

Margie's phone pinged with the special ring she'd set up to alert her that Ed was calling. She smiled. At least one conversation tonight would be pleasant. Her call to her mother had done little more than raise her anxiety level from six to eleven on a scale of one to ten.

She jabbed the ANSWER button and settled in for a chat. "Ed. So nice to hear from you again."

His reply froze her veins. "Sorry, this isn't a pleasure call. Got some bad news."

She sat up and planted her feet on the floor, her heart racing like a runaway horse. "What's going on?"

He filled her in on his meeting with Commander Morgan, each word like another coffin nail pounded into her head. "As you can see, it's better if we don't make contact for a bit."

"How long?" A day without his voice always seemed like a month. How could she stand more than that? "And what about the party?"

"We need to delay the announcement until your name is cleared."

Pound! Pound! Pound!

"And if it isn't?"

"Let's not go there, okay?"

Right. Because if she went to trial and was convicted, prison would be the only way she'd see him again in the foreseeable future.

Oh, God, how am I going to explain this to my parents?

No. She wouldn't let fear take over. Hadn't the pastor preached about that this morning? "Why is he ordering you now? I mean, why not right from the start?"

"They've found more evidence that they think points to you as the killer."

"Such as?"

"Cramer had a note on your application. Denying it."

"How would I know that?"

"They haven't figured that out. An email, phone call, perhaps?"

"But they can look at my phone records. Computer. His. See what he did. They'll see I couldn't possibly have known already." She slapped the coffee table with an open palm. "He wasn't in the office on Friday. Why would he have reviewed it on a Saturday? And then called or emailed me over the weekend? Just to tick me off? No, he was much more likely to let the application languish."

"I agree, Margie. I don't know the man, but I've known some like him. Low-level bureaucrats work passive-aggressively. Ignoring people they don't like."

"But he didn't even know me. Why would he dislike me?"

"True."

A thought struck her. "I'll tell you who doesn't like me, though. Nell at town hall. She has something going with Cramer. She blushed when we talked about him. She gushed about how he was practically a saint. Then coming into the police station and screaming about me threatening him."

"True."

Was that all he could say? "Is it possible she put the note on the application? What did it say?"

"I don't know. Didn't think to ask."

"Could you find out? Maybe it says DENY, rather than DENIED. I'd think there'd be a place for a signature if that was the case. An official stamp, maybe?"

"Good point. I'll see if I can get eyes on."

"Will you let me know?"

"I can't—"

"You still have to walk Bruno, right? How about every evening at six? Sloane's Lake. We could pass each other and whisper or hand over a note. Or set up a drop point to leave information."

He chuckled. "You've been watching too many espionage movies." She longed to touch his face, stare into his eyes. He cleared his throat. "The bench near the south parking lot. Under the tree. We can leave a note there. Nod as you pass if you did, and I'll do the same."

"Sounds like a plan."

"Gotta go. I love you, Margie."

"Love you, too, Copper."

The call disconnected, but she held the phone to her ear for a long while, wishing he were still there.

But wishing never made a thing happen, and this was no different.

She slipped to her knees and did the only thing that could change the past, present, and future.

She prayed.

Chapter 6

Margie's phone buzzed before her alarm on Monday morning. She reached for the device, knocking it off the bedside table, where it hung from its power cord tether like a screen door from one hinge.

"Snap!"

Still-sleepy fingers fumbled for the source of the irritation. When she finally grasped it and yanked it free from the wire, she jabbed at the screen to read the text message.

AM STEPPING IN AS HEAD OF PLANNING COMMITTEE UNTIL WE FIND REPLACEMENT FOR MR. CRAMER. BRINGING NEXT PLANNING MEETING FORWARD TO TONIGHT FOLLOWING TOWN CHRISTMAS PARTY FOR BUSINESS OWNERS. I EXPECT YOU TO ATTEND BOTH. SEE YOU AT THREE. MAYOR JOAN YOUNG, EDGEWATER.

Margie grunted and tossed the phone onto the table. What a nerve! As if she wanted to mingle with the very people who'd already pointed their fingers at her. Then again…

… it could be a great opportunity to suss out possible suspects.

She flung off the covers and completed the task of waking up completely by planting her feet on the cold floor. And since Ed wouldn't be there—her eyes stung, and she swallowed a lump—he couldn't tell her who she could talk to or whose alibi she could poke holes into.

Still, talking about replacing the dead man so soon seemed cold. Calculating, almost. What if the mayor wanted him off the committee? Was that enough reason to kill? She slipped out of her PJs and into her work outfit—jeans with holes in the knees, a t-shirt with old paint splatters, and tennis shoes. Commander Morgan seemed to think a denied application—of which she knew nothing, and he couldn't have proof otherwise—was enough of a reason for murder, so why not a desire to pad an important committee with her own people? She'd check into other plans and property deals in the town, see if Madam Mayor had reasons to off Cramer.

JoJo refused to be ignored another second, so Margie led them twice around the lake at a quick walk/slow job change-out. By the time they arrived home, both were ready for breakfast. Dog first, then her. In about thirty seconds, the pup inhaled her food, then flopped onto her doggie bed. Eyes drooped, and she was soon asleep.

Feeling only a little jealous at the Lab's lack of anything else important to do, Margie made a quick breakfast of cold cereal, toast, and coffee. She jotted a note into her phone to pick up more milk so she could enjoy the same gourmet repast the next day, then headed down to the shop, travel mug in hand.

When she unlocked the door into the retail area, chill air greeted her. Like the inside of a burial vault, all dank and dusty.

She shivered and turned up the thermostat before flipping on the lights. A quick check outside the front door confirmed the overnight winds had swept away every leaf in sight, so she didn't have to sweep the sidewalk today. Which was good, since when she did, she invariably met one of the other business owners, and right now, she was in no mood to talk to anybody. Or answer any more questions.

Yes, siree. A quiet morning in the shop, setting up the display for her upcoming book event, was just what the doctor ordered.

If she'd needed a doctor, that is.

No, right now she needed a good friend on whose shoulder she could cry.

She inhaled, straightened her shoulders, and set her cup on the display case. She didn't have any shoulder on which to lay her head, so instead she'd jump into the next best form of therapy—work.

First, find a table or other surface. After scouring the storage and back rooms, she dragged a scarred wooden piece about the size of a card table into the shop area. By shoving her seating area closer to the window and moving a magazine rack into a corner, she cleared enough room so customers wouldn't trip over themselves when the entered.

She studied the space. Four books, one for each week. So, about a quarter of the table per. The first book, *Adventure at the Grange*, an early Doyle work featuring

66

Sherlock Holmes, needed a background of some sort. Margie studied what she had available. Perhaps she should have given this more thought, rather than depending on the what's-on-hand model of decorating.

Ah! That was perfect. An old timey table easel made from wrought iron. Black. Cold. Indefatigable. Open to the page where he first uttered those famous words, "Come, Watson. The game is afoot." A quick visit to the cash register produced an empty bullet casing she'd found on the path around the lake and kept for no reason. Fit the setting because in this book, the lord of the manor dies by gunshot. On a pad of paper, she scribbled two items: wooden pipe. Deerstalker hat.

Sounded like a trip to a thrift store was in order.

But first she'd complete the other three sections of the display in case she identified more items needed.

The second book, *The Mysterious Affair at Styles*, one of her favorite Poirot tales, features a lady of the manor who dies by strychnine. While she had a tiny vial of the poison on hand—what self-respecting mystery bookstore wouldn't have an antique medicine cabinet on display, duly locked and secured? Still, she had several empty vials she could fill with something harmless like baking soda that would look enough like the real thing to send a shiver down the spine of any Christie aficionado. A trip upstairs provided those two items, along with a fancy lace fan, a pair of kidskin evening gloves, and a dainty pearled hair comb for good measure. She opened the book and set the items inside it. Nice.

Book three, *The Big Sleep*, posed a bit of a problem. The plot involved pornography and blackmail, and she had no intention of bringing nasty pictures into her shop. Still, she had an old typewriter. Maybe she could produce the beginnings of a blackmail letter, prop the book against the machine, and perhaps some of those fake bills she'd seen at a local discount store recently. Add another item to the shopping list: play money.

The final volume, *Hawksmoor*, might prove easier. Set in the 1970s, this story recounted a series of murders set two hundred years before, which were being replicated in the present. Linked to an architect and a set of six churches he built, perhaps she could do with a set of blueprints—she had the ones for the addition to her shop—a cross, and a piece of piano wire. Although where she'd find that, she hadn't a clue. She shrugged. Add it to the list. Perhaps something else would serve as a substitution.

When her stomach grumbled, she checked the clock. Goodness. Half-past one. She barely had time for a quick shower, lunch, then dress to head to the town Christmas party. If she left early, maybe she'd have time to stop off and get the items to complete her display.

Except the fates conspired against her again. When she reached the top of the steps, JoJo rushed toward her, tail wagging, lead in her mouth.

Margie sighed. "Come on. Let's do this quick. I don't think Mayor Young will accept a tardy slip from me signed by my dog."

An abbreviated round of the neighborhood, and they arrived back home out of breath. Another scoop of food for her four-legged housemate, then Margie slipped into the shower, soaped up her hair, and worked to wash away all her troubles and worries.

If only.

{*}

At five past three, made late because she stopped to call the towing company to remove a Black Lexus parked in her lot—might as well take advantage of the service while setting a precedent that the lot belonged to her—Margie entered the community hall and paused. At least two hundred people milled about filled the small space, leaving little room to move. Chairs lined the walls, most occupied. A white foil Christmas tree in the far corner screamed a distinct lack of taste, while a song including Santa and stockings and toys played from the tinny and overworked sound system.

A knot of business owners parted before her like she was the bow of the Titanic, leaving a gaping hole in the crowd about wide enough to sail the Grand Old Lady through. Several turned up their noses at her, giving her the cold shoulder. One whispered from behind her hand to a grouping of three others, who broke into a cackle resembling the hens kept by her across-the-alley neighbor.

She headed for the drink table and asked the young man filling orders for a sparkling water with lime, which he promptly handed her. Turning to face the melee before her, she sipped her beverage, watching the crowd

69

over the rim of the glass. Bubbles tickled her nose, and ice cubes clinked against her front teeth as though begging for escape from their confines.

Mayor Young appeared in front of her as though she'd popped up from a hole in the floor, then gripped her painfully by the elbow. "So glad you made it, Marjie, dear. Come over here. I simply must introduce you to my friends."

Finding no way to escape the woman's butchering of her name or her clutches, Margie followed, feeling much like a sheep being led to the slaughter. Who were these friends? And why did Ms. Mayor think Margie wanted to meet them? Or they her?

Five women dressed in power suits and stilettos occupied a patch of floor big enough for a postage stamp. They separated as Mayor Young breezed into their midst, Margie trailing behind.

The mayor, who Margie now noticed slurred several words, mumbled out the names of the women, pointing to each. "Camilla Harris." A tall, leggy redhead. "Hetty Walsh." A lithe blonde whose hair Mother Nature never colored. "Alice Gonzales." Beautiful woman with dark eyes that bored into her soul. "Janice Morris." Older than the rest, with thick spectacles and a slightly vague expression. Disinterest? Amusement? Too much red wine? "And last but not least, my assistant, Cathy."

Margie nodded to each, holding her tongue. Interesting that the secretary didn't warrant a surname. And that the mayor never revealed their relationship to her. "I'm Margie Hanson. I own the Mysterious Ink Mystery Bookstore on 26th."

Janice's eyebrows, carefully waxed, then penciled in, rose and disappeared under her fringe. "Oh, how nice. I've heard book sales have dropped recently."

Business she could talk all day. "Actually, quite the opposite—"

The mayor clicked her tongue. "Girls, girls." All turned to her like obedient students. "No shop talk today. We're here to party."

The mayor's desire to nip the conversation in the bud probably had less to do with quenching the party spirit than the fact said Ms. Mayor preferred to control the discussion. Margie sipped her seltzer and studied the dynamics of the group, quickly confirming her supposition about Mayor Young's desire to be in the spotlight.

A couple of minutes into a monologue by the mayor sharing rumors about a mutual acquaintance of the others, somebody bumped Margie from behind as she focused on the details. She took a couple of steps forward, running into the mayor, who dropped her drink on the floor.

The glass shattered, splashing liquid on the others. One of them—Janice, perhaps—squealed and stepped back, jostling another guest. Soon, a chain reaction of spilled drinks, body contact, and apologies filtered around the room like a bizarre wave.

Margie squatted down and picked up the larger

pieces of broken glass. Using a tissue from her purse, she mopped up the liquid as best she could, avoiding the shards that would puncture easily.

When she stood, the mayor's brow pulled down. "What do you think you're doing?"

"I'm sorry." Heat rose to Margie's cheeks. She hated being the center of attention. She shouldn't have come at all. "Somebody pushed me."

Rising on her toes, the mayor called to the other attendees. "Did anybody see who pushed her? Come on. 'Fess up." When nobody moved or replied, she turned back to Margie. "I think you've had too much to drink, girlie."

"But it's only—"

Mayor Young snapped her fingers. "Fetch me another. A G&T large. No ice."

Wishing she could tap her heels and disappear, Margie trotted to the drink table and asked for the mayor's choice.

The young man gestured to a tray of drinks before him. "Be just a minute. Got about ten mixers ahead of you."

"No worries. Back in a minute."

Glad to have time to dash into the ladies' room for a moment to herself, Margie headed that direction. Thankfully, she was alone, so she washed her hands, patted cool water on her cheeks, and reapplied her lip gloss. A couple of deep breaths, then she counted to ten and returned to the party.

A different bartender nodded at the glass sitting at the end of the prep area, the lights glinting off his copper-colored hair. "That's for the lady mayor."

Margie thanked him and took the glass, then wove her way through the partygoers, some of whom seemed to have taken root on the floor. After handing off the drink, she waited awkwardly for the group to move on and leave her standing there.

If only.

Instead, they all seemed content to occupy their particular piece of real estate. Cathy chattered on about her wedding plans, while the other women rolled their eyes and focused on several couples slow-dancing.

The mayor, tired of not being the focus, swirled the ice cubes with a forefinger, which she then licked. "Well, ladies. Let's see what the food is like." She coughed. "Sorry. Something in my throat." A long swig of gin and tonic followed. "Ah, that's better."

Another cough. A rasping noise like furniture moving across a wooded floor. The mayor clutched her throat. Her neck arched back. The glass fell from frozen fingers.

And the woman fell to the floor.

Eyes wide open.

A single shuddering breath.

Gone.

Chapter 7

Janice pointed at her, her face writhing. "It's her. She's the murderer." She stepped back. "She poisoned the mayor."

A circle of onlooker gathered round, pressing together, creating a wall of bodies with her and the now-dead mayor in the center, like an evil game of Ring Around the Rosey. Margie looked for a way out, but the businesspeople of Edgewater could have been the defensive line for the Patriots, so tightly woven were they.

The woman who'd turned up her nose at her as she entered the party and then sidestepped her, as though afraid of contamination, now appeared in her line of vision. "She's the woman who killed dear Earl Cramer, you know." She swiveled her head toward a shorter woman beside her. "Nell here knows all about her. Told the police they shouldn't trust her. Don't know what they're thinking, letting a killer out on the loose."

Two men standing behind Margie stepped forward and gripped her wrists. She wrestled with them, then gave up. Making a scene wouldn't help her case any. She leaned toward Janice, who'd seemed the friendliest to her, in a distant sort of way. "Please call the police. And the paramedics. Just in case she isn't—"

"Murdered?" Cathy, her eyes filled with tears and

her nose red, thrust her face into Margie's. "Of course, she is. It's what you wanted, isn't it?"

"No, I never—"

"Yeah, that's what you said when they arrested you for killing Mr. Cramer."

"No, they didn't—"

"Well, you killed him, didn't you?"

"No. I found him—"

"That's what they all say, isn't it?" Cathy whirled to face the crowd again. "Just like on television." She used air quotes that encapsulated her next statement in sarcasm. "Not them. They're innocent." She faced Margie and waggled a forefinger at her. "But the police caught you holding the murder weapon."

The accusation and harsh words hung in the still air of the now-stuffy room. "Please, call the police."

Her head swirled, and if not for the men holding her arms, she might have fallen. Her knees buckled, and she took a step forward to catch herself.

Cathy snatched at this and ran with it like a dog stealing a steak from a neighborhood party grill. "Hold on to her, guys. Don't let her get away. You'll be heroes in the paper tomorrow."

A camera nearby flashed, blinding Margie for an instant. Off to her right, a man held up his cell phone in the classic video pose.

Great, he'll sell that to a television station and make a bundle.

She twisted her hand, wrenching it from her

75

captor's grip, and stretched out for the offending phone, missing by inches.

Cathy's caterwaul picked up again. "Don't let her get away. She's a wild one. Look at her eyes. Like a rabid dog, she is."

Muttering from the attenders rose, and bodies mashed against each other. Hands from those behind groped at her arms, her hair. One touched her jacket and pulled.

Her hand pried fingers loose. "Stop it. You have no right."

A burly man with a military cut and bearing stepped into the middle of the circle with her and the body. He held up a hand. "Folks. Step back. I'll take over from here."

The second man, squishing her wrist to mush, frowned. "Who are you?"

"Private security hired for the party."

"How do we know you won't help her escape?"

The ex-Marine type pulled identification from his chest pocket. "Rick Stone, Blackstone Security."

Janice peered at him, then turned to Cathy. "Do you know this guy?"

Cathy's shoulders slumped a fraction. "Mayor Young hired him. He's legit."

Mr. Stone took control of the situation when the others stepped back. "You. Come with me."

Hetty shook her head. "You're not taking her out of our sight. The police are on their way. I'm sure they'll have plenty of questions. You don't have any legal standing here."

Margie eyed the woman with renewed interest. An attorney? Or a legal clerk wannabe? Still, she wasn't certain she wanted to go anywhere with this man. She stood her ground. "I'll wait here, if you don't mind."

Stone's brow pulled down. "Ma'am, I was hoping you'd sit over here in the corner where I can keep you safe."

Camilla chose this moment to butt in. "And keep an eye on her, too. Don't forget that little detail." She peered at him. "Or are you one of those department store cops who likes to dress up in a uniform and play like an actual police officer?"

"I don't forget details." Stone sneered. "I also don't overstep my purview. And if you'll notice, I'm plain-suit. Never liked uniforms. Too constrictive."

Margie bit her lip to hold back her smile. Camilla's cheeks burned red, and she snorted and melted back into the crowd.

Cathy pointed to a grouping of chairs in a corner. "Over there work for you?"

Mr. Stone nodded. "Thanks for your help. Ma'am?"

Well, so long as they stayed in this room, she should be safe.

Actually, until she rested in her own bed again, she'd never feel entirely secure.

{*}

Ed pulled up in his car and stepped out. Three officers from Edgewater wandered around the outside of the community center, and a sergeant stood at the door, a clipboard in hand.

Ed nodded to him. "Sarge."

"Detective Hogan. You drew the short straw tonight?"

"I did. What's going on?"

"Dead body inside. Suspect in custody. Private security has control for now. Lakewood PD are on call if we need them."

"Thanks, Sarge." Edgewater's Police Department had just enough officers to patrol a medium-sized funeral, and not much more. Thankfully, surrounding departments often lent them bodies and resources as needed. He breathed deep. "Into the fray."

"Better you than me." He pointed to a line on the sheet held to his clipboard. "Sign here."

As recorder of the crime scene, the sergeant notated who entered and left the building. Helped maintain the integrity of the area, as well as double-checked that everyone was out when the doors were sealed and assisted with report writing and witness interviews.

Ed signed on the second line. The first line contained the name and signature of the patrol officer who responded to the call for service and arrived on the scene first. Thankfully, the short list meant police boots hadn't muddied the crime scene. Figuratively speaking, of course. No telling what mess those already at the scene might have made.

In the door and a sharp left into the large community area where most events took place. Typical layout, apart from the ugly plastic tree in the corner. A small bar, complete with a black-vested bartender and plenty of empty glasses. To the left, a door marked RESTROOMS. Plastic chairs lining the walls. A grouping of dozens hovering and talking amongst themselves.

A well-built man in his mid-thirties approached. "Rick Stone of Blackstone Security. Private gig tonight."

"Ed Hogan, Edgewater PD." The two shook hands, and Ed sized the man up. He wouldn't want to meet him in a dark alley unless Stone fought on his side. "You took custody of the suspect?"

He shook his head. "Not really. Let's say I rescued her from the wolves that wanted to tear her apart, limb from limb."

"Well, thanks. Never looks good when the media finds out we tossed a suspect to the dogs before we even book them."

Stone stepped aside and gestured to a chair against the wall. "She's sitting over there. I'm off duty now. All yours."

Ed eyed the woman hunched in the chair, turned to bid the agent good evening, then froze. Slowly he swiveled his head back to the suspect.

No, it can't be.

He stared. "Margie."

79

"Beg your pardon, sir?"

Ed turned to the private security guy. "Huh?"

"You said something. Sounded like a name."

"Never mind. Talking to myself. Good night."

So, how to handle this? Businesslike? Every cell screamed at him to run to her and wrap her in his arms, assure her this was all a nightmare and they'd both wake up and laugh about it. Except he couldn't. By rights, he should march right out, call Commander Morgan and apprise him of the situation, then take himself home.

He absolutely should not go over there and commence the investigation. Any evidence he found—whether mitigating or not—would be questioned at any level. And if the press learned of his involvement, Margie wouldn't stand a chance of a fair hearing of any kind.

She glanced up, caught his eye, and her mouth opened partway, as though she might call out his name. Then she clamped her lips shut and shoved her shoulders back.

She knows. She understands why I can't simply whisk her away.

So he'd do what he came here for. Take her in for questioning. Assign officers to interview witnesses. Then hand her over to Commander Morgan, who wouldn't be pleased at being called in.

That would make three of them.

Four if he counted Mayor Young.

{*}

Margie's head pounded in time with the clanging of cell

doors, echoing off the walls of the room, drowning out the words of the police officer opposite her.

She stared, unable—or perhaps unwilling—to comprehend him. All she could hear were Ed's clipped words when he'd approached her at the community center.

"Come with me. Don't say a word."

"Are you arresting me?"

"I don't have a choice."

"Please take my keys and check on JoJo."

"Don't worry. I'll see to her. Now follow me."

Not wanting to make things more difficult for him—as if they weren't already awkward enough—she did as he said. Riding to the station in the rear seat of his car, she'd tried a couple of times to ask questions. Each time, a curt shake of his head and a frown were his only responses.

At the station, he'd led her into the same interrogation room she'd occupied just two days before. Almost exactly forty-eight hours—was that possible? She'd sat, hands in her lap, even though this time he'd refrained from cuffing her. Still, iron shackles, waist belt, and handcuffs couldn't have weighed more heavily than the tons of worry that now sat on her shoulders.

Then he'd left her—again—and his superior officer strode in.

That was an hour ago. Morgan was civil enough— no waterboarding or threats of beatings in his repertoire. Instead, he laid out the evidence clearly and concisely, as well as the plan for the investigation of yet another crime in which she featured foremost.

He flipped through the contents of a file folder. "You'll spend the night here with us. Tomorrow, we have a polygraph scheduled."

"We both know you can't use the results in court."

He eyed her. "True. But we can see where we both stand once we have that."

"I didn't kill her. I didn't kill Cramer." She leaned forward. "I'm really tired, and I want to go home." She swallowed back the Texas-sized lump in her throat. "Charge me or release me."

"We can hold you for up to forty-eight hours pending the results of our investigation."

"You won't find any evidence against me if you hold me for forty-eight years."

He chuckled. "Might have to do that. Soon as you're found guilty."

She leaned back, her shoulders sagging. "But I'm not."

He scanned the pages. "We have several witnesses who say you did."

"All friends of the mayor, no doubt."

"Not the bartender."

She sat up. "Right. I ordered the mayor's drink from one guy, but somebody else was there when I came back from the restroom. Which one did you talk to?"

"The one who fixed the drink."

"Describe him."

"Stocky, I guess I'd call him. Lanky hair falling into his face."

"That's the first guy. What about the carrot top who gave me the glass?"

Another check of the contents of the file. "Nobody there by that description." He snapped the folder shut. "At any rate, he said you ordered her drink. And you picked it up."

"Sure, but it was sitting there for several minutes before I did."

"Not according to him. And you carried it back to the mayor, giving you opportunity to slip something in."

"And my motive?"

"She was stepping in as head of the planning committee. You hadn't expected that. Maybe you thought the committee would languish until they found somebody else."

"Which wouldn't have done me any good. I want to get my addition started right away. No decision wasn't to my benefit."

He shrugged. "Maybe you didn't like the mayor or her politics."

"I don't kill everybody I don't agree with. Or else I'd be really busy picking folks off."

"We also have several witnesses who say you knocked the mayor's first drink out of her hand. Seems like you set everything up perfectly."

"Somebody bumped or pushed me from behind.

It wasn't intentional on my part."

"One witness said she thought the move was exceptionally intentional. Almost like you'd staged it."

Margie sniffed. "Cathy, right? The adoring assistant?"

"Actually, no. Alice Gonzales."

"What killed the mayor?"

"You should know."

"Well, if I did, I wouldn't have to ask, would I?"

"Same stuff as is in the vial on display in your shop."

Her heart sank. "You broke into my store? Did you have a search warrant?"

"We did." He held up a tri folded paper marked WARRANT. "We tried not to disturb anything, but the vial of strychnine in your display cabinet confirmed our suspicions."

"It's just that. A display. I bought it at a yard sale."

"And what about that macabre set-up with the vial on the table?"

"Baking powder, if you checked it."

"Actually, we did. And you're right, it is." He pushed a plastic evidence bag containing another vial across the table. "But what about this?"

She peered at the item. "What is it?"

He turned the bag over and pointed to the words scribbled in the spaces.

She blinked.

This couldn't be happening to her.

LOCATION FOUND: MARGIE HANSON'S JACKET POCKET.

PRESUMPTIVE TEST SUGGESTS CONTENTS ARE STRYCHNINE.

Chapter 8

Tuesday morning, Margie awoke, stiff and chilled. The fluorescent lights overhead flickered and crackled as though protesting the rude awakening on her behalf. If she'd had more energy and a gallon of coffee, she'd smile.

As it was, since she had neither, she followed the female officer to a room marked POLYGRAPH. Another woman waited inside behind a machine which vomited a multitude of cables and wires, as well as a chair that vaguely resembled an electric chair in an old timey movie.

She sat when directed and shivered, keeping her gaze on the floor. Deep breaths helped calm her nerves, but did nothing for her sweating palms, which she swiped on her pants leg.

The tester smiled. "I'm Rachel Burwin. I'll be doing your test today. There's nothing to worry about. Just relax while I connect you to Old Bertha here."

"Bertha?"

"Figured if I gave her a name, she wouldn't seem so intimidating."

After attaching a strap around her chest and a device similar to an oximeter to her finger, Ms. Burwin nodded. "You're doing great." A skinny needle on a roll of paper traced a jagged line on a screen. "I'm going to ask you two questions as a base. Answer truthfully on the first and lie on the second. Okay?"

Margie nodded.

"Name?"

"Margie Hanson."

"Date of birth?"

"Um, June 14th, 1900."

The needle jumped drastically.

"Good. Shall we begin?"

An hour later, Margie breathed deep through her nose as Rachel removed the tracers. "How did I do?"

"I'm sorry. I can't disclose that. Commander Morgan will receive my report in a couple of days."

Margie's brow pulled down. "I didn't see any issues. Did you?"

The tester smiled at her. "Let's just say, you seem to be a very honest person."

Seem to be? What did she mean by that? "Can you fool these machines?"

"I've had some questionable results when a person is very nervous. Or is skirting the truth but not exactly lying."

Margie snorted. "I read once about a guy who put a thumbtack in his shoe. He tricked the machine by lying and pressing his heel into the tack."

"That's an old wives' tale."

"I have nothing to lie about. It's not like you asked me my opinion about the current political climate."

Rachel giggled. "Funny." She nodded toward the door. "An officer is waiting outside for you. Good luck."

Luck? If she didn't have bad luck, she'd have none. Who else but her could be on the scene of two separate murders in two days? Nobody but Grandma Carly, that's for sure.

When she exited the room, the same officer from earlier waited for her. She pulled a set of handcuffs from her duty belt. "Sorry, but you're going to court. Preliminary charges, and maybe a bond hearing, too."

Margie held her hands in front of her. "You're just doing your job."

"Thank you." The young woman gripped her elbow. "Down this way."

After a brief ride in the backseat of a patrol car—her third in two days—they arrived at the town's courthouse. Inside, she waited in a cell with four women who studiously ignored her. One occupied the only chair, chomping on her fingernails, while the others alternated between pacing the floor and leaning against a wall. She kept her gaze down, praying her docket came up first.

It didn't. Third, however, was better than fifth.

As she stepped through the door leading to the defendant's table, she scanned the courtroom. Ed sat in the row behind the district attorney, alongside Commander Morgan. She tossed him a tentative smile, but his expression didn't change. Stoic. Staring straight ahead.

A middle-aged man sat to her right. He turned and offered his hand. "Jake Chavez. Public defender. I've read your file. Plead not guilty if you're asked. Hopefully we can get you out of here on bond. Do you have security?"

A sarcastic response bubbled up, which Margie swallowed back. "I do. A bookstore and house."

"Good. Ties to the community. Family?"

"Not here."

"Too bad. Oh, well, I'll put the best spin on it I can." A door behind the judge's desk opened, and a woman stepped out dressed in a black robe. Mr. Chavez nodded in that direction. "Judge McLean. She's fair but tough. Hope for the best. Pray if you do."

Margie nodded. Seemed prayer was the only thing she could do right now.

The district attorney offered his three witnesses: first on scene officer, who relayed about finding the body. Commander Morgan, who explained about the strychnine. Mr. Chavez asked a few questions intended to elicit information about other potential suspects but appeared to make little headway. Then the bailiff called Ed.

As he approached the witness stand, he glanced her direction. His mouth turned down and his shoulders slumped. Had he given up on her? Did he now believe her guilty? Or was he apologizing in advance for his testimony?

She tied her fingers into knots in her lap.

Mr. Chavez leaned close. "You know him?"

She nodded. "Unofficially engaged."

"Ouch."

Her breath caught in her throat. "But please don't bring it up. I don't want his career jeopardized."

"Might raise questions about his part in the investigation."

"Please."

The DA asked questions about Earl Cramer's death. About finding her kneeling over the body, the murder weapon in her hand.

Thud! Thud! Nails in her coffin again.

Mr. Chavez rose, and Margie gripped his shirtsleeve, then shook her head. He smiled down at her, then addressed Ed. "Detective Hogan, isn't it true that the witnesses in this first case exaggerated my client's words?"

"Yes, a little."

"And you talked with witnesses to the unfortunate death of the mayor?"

"I did."

"And what did they say?"

Ed shifted in his seat, glanced at her, then away. "Most saw nothing."

He's trying to protect me. Oh, God, don't let him destroy his career.

"But some did?"

Apparently, her public defender was like a bulldog with a bone. Whose side was he on?

Ed cleared his throat, swallowed hard a couple of time, then nodded. Once.

Mr. Chavez peered at him. "Come now,

Detective. You know you need to verbalize your response for the record."

Judge McLean tapped her gavel on the desk. "I will admonish the witness, Mr. Chavez, when needed." She smiled down at Ed. "But he is correct. Please speak your answers."

"Yes. Several witnesses told me that M—the defendant intentionally bumped the mayor, spilling her drink. Then offered to get her another."

Margie gasped. Not true. Or was it? Is that how it happened? Had she merely been polite and offered to replace the beverage? She wasn't certain any longer.

"Anything else, Detective, that you want to add?"

"Such as?"

"Did you believe the witnesses?"

"They seemed forthright in what they said. They truly believed what they thought they saw."

"But they could be wrong?"

"Possibly."

"Isn't it true, Detective Hogan, that eyewitness testimony is notoriously skewed according to what the person thinks they saw?"

"Sometimes. Which is why we look for corroborating facts."

"Such as?"

"Multiple witnesses with the same evidence."

"Did you have that in this case?"

Ed lifted his chin. "We did."

"And if those witnesses had a reason to skew their

testimony?"

"Did they?" Her fiancé's cheeks turned red. "I'm not aware of that."

"Well, for example, the clerk at the town hall who overheard my client as she left the office. She—shall we say—added to my client's words, didn't she?"

"She might have—"

"Exaggerated. Yes. Did she have an ulterior motive to do that?"

"I don't know. I didn't ask her. I'm not privy to the case notes."

Mr. Chavez took a step closer. "And why is that?"

No, please. Don't ask him…

"I'm working on other cases."

"On whose orders?"

The district attorney stood. "Objection, Your Honor. What cases this detective is working on and why is no concern of this court."

Judge McLean's lips pursed. "He is your witness, Mr. DA. You must believe he has relevant information for this case. If he's not actively involved, why is he here?"

"I called him only for the purpose of bringing in evidence from the initial case against this defendant."

Mr. Chavez whirled to face the judge. "A charge which has not come before the Court yet, Your Honor. For which she is still presumed innocent until proven guilty."

The judge nodded. "Yet could be considered

evidence of prior behavior."

"She is not guilty."

"So say you. And probably Ms. Hanson as well. I think I've heard enough. Objection sustained." The judge nodded and Mr. Chavez returned to sit beside Margie. "Bail is set at five hundred thousand dollars. You can make arrangements with the bailiff. The clerk will provide the preliminary hearing date by end of day. Thank you."

The bailiff stood. "All rise."

Margie raised herself on shaky legs as the judge left through the same door behind the bench. Then she sank to her seat again. Pulled the chain holding her engagement ring out from under her sweater. Undid the clasp, allowing the ring to rest in her palm.

Mr. Chavez gripped her elbow. "Stick close to me. We'll get the bail thing done and we'll slip out the back door just in case the press is waiting out front."

She nodded and together they headed out of the courtroom, he on her right. As they passed the district attorney's desk, she slowed and made eye contact with Ed. He opened his mouth, then snapped it shut and dropped his gaze.

She leaned as close as she could without drawing undue attention and slipped her hand into his. His eyes widened, then he held his hand out.

The ring.

No longer hers.

As he was no longer her fiancé, either.

Chapter 9

When Margie awoke the next morning, her fingers went to where her ring once rested at the base of her neck, but they came away empty. Almost as empty as her heart.

The emotions of the previous day swept over her once more. The abject fear. Breath-stealing court appearance. Hearing Ed's words highlighted the dire situation she found herself in. Made her realize that trying to fool herself into thinking she could maintain their relationship and not endanger his career was foolishness.

No. Ending it now was better. No matter how all this turned out, things could never be the same between them.

Could they?

JoJo's cold nose poked under the covers, reminding her that even though her love life had evaporated into thin air, her dog still needed her. As would her business. Although she'd given the title as security for her bail, customers would expect her to open the doors as usual.

Or would they? A few faces came to mind who wouldn't believe she could be a killer—even an unintentional one. But no doubt more than a few looky-loos might make an appearance in the coming days. And possibly one or two outright accusers.

She tossed the blankets aside and slid her feet into slippers before petting the dog. One thing she had to admit: Ed had taken good care of the pup while she wasn't available.

"Walk after I shower."

Exhausted by her ordeal, she'd collapsed into bed the evening before, but now couldn't stand the still-lingering smell of the jail cells. What was it about urine, bleach, unwashed bodies, and cheap perfume—not hers—that lingered?

Under the water, which drowned out her thoughts, she imagined all her problems spinning down the drain along with the soap and shampoo bubbles. Maybe if she stood here long enough, they would slough off like dry skin, leaving her feeling soft and new.

But when she stepped out and dried off, the reality of her circumstances struck her once more. She sank onto the toilet lid, breathing deep as black spots threatened at the outer edges of her vision. JoJo licked her hand, then sank at her feet, panting and looking up at her, a furrow of worry between her eyes.

She forced a smile. "We'll be okay, girl. Let's get this day on the go, shall we?"

While blow-drying her hair, she offered prayers for the families of both Cramer and the mayor. No matter who killed them, their loved ones were left to pick up the pieces.

The biggest problem was that as long as Commander Morgan remained convinced she was the murderer, he wouldn't look for anybody else. Which meant that person would get away with it.

Until they made a mistake.

Maybe she should stay home and not venture out. Keep the shop closed.

No. She had a huge promotion going on this week. Promises made to customers. Book binding repairs to complete. Special orders to prepare and mail. People depending on her.

Not to mention JoJo demanded her exercise. And she needed to do something other than wallow in fear and worry, including a business to run. Because one thing was certain: Once this was over, she'd continue in business.

If she had one to continue.

As she dressed, her cell rang. *Ed.* Should she answer or let it go to voicemail?

She waited, her heart longing to talk to him, but afraid of what he might say. Then again, hadn't she put the period at the end of their relationship yesterday by returning his ring?

Her voicemail picked up. She pulled on jeans and socks, a sweatshirt to ward off the chill in the shop when the door opened—if it opened—then tied her hair back with a scrunchie. A ping alerted her to a message.

She tapped the button.

Hi Margie. It's me.

As if she'd forgotten the sound of his voice already.

Listen, I'm sorry for what happened in court yesterday. I

didn't come off as if I believe you. But I do. In both cases.

She hoped he'd be on her jury when the cases came to trial. Although, of course, he wouldn't.

I'd love to get together again. I don't want this to be the end. I know why you gave me back the ring yesterday. But I won't accept that we have no future.

Well, Ed Hogan, you might have to do just that.

Can we meet at that little coffee shop in Green Mountain? The one in the strip mall at Jewell and Union? At nine? Bring JoJo, and I'll bring Bruno. They miss each other.

She detected the hint of longing in his voice that mirrored the cry of her heart. Maybe they weren't as over as she'd thought. Perhaps they could still be friends. See where this went once she was exonerated.

If you're not there, I'll have my answer.

She checked the clock. Just enough time to feed the pup, walk her around the parking lot to do her first business of the day, and get there. Her breaths came shallow and quick, like a teen on her first date.

Seemed like her head hadn't communicated to her heart that there was no future for them. Then her grandmother's words surfaced: So long as there is life, there is hope.

That's exactly what she needed to hear. She'd given up believing that God could fix this. It was too big, too complicated, right? For the Lord of the universe? Surely it hadn't caught Him by surprise, even though it had shocked the socks off her.

She grabbed a jacket and the leash, called to the

dog, and trotted down the stairs. In the lot, she noted the illegally parked car was gone.

Fast work, EZ Riders.

Then she loaded JoJo into the car and headed toward Green Mountain.

Despite a niggling in a corner of her heart to take it slow, she wouldn't keep him waiting.

{*}

Ed shifted in his chair in the recent addition to the coffee shop, vying for a better view of the parking lot. He checked the clock on the wall behind the barista. Five 'til. Would she come? Had she even listened to his message? Did she believe him?

He prayed the answer to each of those questions was a resounding YES. If not—well, what could he do? He'd accept her absence as her final say in the matter. Kinda like that old song from the 70s about knocking three times on the ceiling, twice on the pipes if the answer is no. Somehow, if she tapped twice, he'd get on with his life.

Or try to.

Face it, Hogan. Losing her wasn't like losing a favorite sweater. This was bone deep. Life-changing.

Bruno, lying beneath the table, bounded to his feet and whimpered. Ed looked up. The most beautiful woman in the world and her charcoal-colored dog stood in the doorway.

He felt like a man whose death sentence was commuted. Perhaps she'd even pardon him.

Ed resisted rushing over to her, choosing to let her make her move. She placed and received her coffee, then crossed the store and sat across from him. JoJo licked his hand, then turned her attentions to Bruno, greeting him as though they'd been apart for a week rather than just the day before.

He quirked his chin at the pups. "They've got the right idea."

She pursed her lips. "They don't have many worries. Don't concern themselves with what others think or say."

He reached across the table, but she pulled her hand out of reach, busying herself with removing her gloves and slipping off her jacket. Designed to give her a few extra seconds to figure out what to say, he surmised. As he would, in her situation.

Except as the man who loved her, he was, in a way. Going through this heartache with her. Knowing she was innocent—rather, believing—her predicament tore at his heart.

She looked around. "This is nice."

"Thanks. I come here sometimes when I need a place where I wouldn't run into anybody I knew."

A smile lifted the corners of her mouth. "Other beautiful women, you mean?" She held up a hand. "Not sure I want to know."

He shook his head. Seemed her sense of humor was on the rebound. "No. CI's. Confidential informants. Or setting up a sting with officers from other jurisdictions."

"Oh, like undercover stuff?"

"Sometimes. And occasionally, when I wanted to be alone with my thoughts."

"Hopefully nobody will poke their fingers in my face and accuse me of murder."

He detected sadness in her tone and her words. Maybe the light-hearted banter was a cover. "I can't even imagine how tough this has been for you."

"And you." She held his gaze. "I want to explain why I gave back your ring."

"No need. I know why."

Her head tilted in question. "You do?"

"Yes. You want a bigger stone, right?"

She rewarded his efforts with a half-smile. "Right. You saw through me." She sipped her coffee, then set the cup down, leaving her hand within reach. "I don't want you to get in trouble because of me."

"Well, you're too late." This time, when he covered her hand with his, she didn't flinch or withdraw. "I'm already in deep trouble."

Her eyes widened. "No. Tell me it isn't so."

He forced his face to remain still. "Absolutely. You have stolen my heart, and if you don't at least give me some assurance there is a future for us when this is over, I will dry up and die, like a leaf falling from a tree in November."

She snorted. "Such melodrama. You missed your calling. You should be on the stage."

100

"Well, this is no fiction story, milady. Please say you'll give me another chance."

Her eyes filled, and her bottom lip trembled.

"Please."

She nodded, and a single tear slipped down her cheek. "I'll try. But I can't promise anything. As you said, my world is inside a hamster wheel right now. And I'm running full speed ahead, trying to escape, but there's no way to get off. You know?"

He didn't, but he would try.

"Thanks, Ed, for being a good friend."

Not fiancé. Not lover. Just friend.

That would do. For now.

{*}

When Ed's cell phone rang, Margie almost groaned. What a way to end such a gut-wrenching moment. Then again, he was a cop. What did she expect? He was a cop. She was a suspect. By God's grace, this would not always be their lot in life.

He turned his shoulder to her and lowered his voice after the initial greeting. Still, that didn't keep her from overhearing a couple of phrases. "When?" "I know of him. Never been in there." He glanced her way. "Well, you can cross her off the suspect list for this one. She's here with me. Has been for almost an hour." He frowned. "I am keeping my distance, sir." Another grimace. "Understood." He ended the call. "Sorry."

"Commander Morgan?"

"Yep."

"Bad news?"

"Another murder. Bart Elgin. Know him?"

"No. Who is he?"

He peered into her eyes. "I wouldn't have thought you did, given his line of business."

"Which is?"

"A pornography shop. Or, as he'd call it, an adult entertainment store. They sell—"

"I know the kind of stuff they carry." She shuddered. "As I said, never been there. No reason to."

"No, of course not."

"So, did your commander think it could have been me?"

"Yes, until I told him you were with me at the time."

"Who is this guy?"

"Apart from his nasty chain of stores, we've suspected for years he's had connections with the mob."

"Stop teasing me. We have mafia in Denver?"

"Actually, throughout Colorado. Pueblo was once mafia headquarters. The Smaldone family once controlled Denver. Still has a stranglehold over several industries, including porn, prostitution, and drugs."

"I never knew."

"Most people don't. When they hear mafia, they think Al Capone and the Untouchables and prohibition."

"So why would Commander Morgan think I was involved? Except, of course, clearing three cases by charging me would be a feather in his cap."

"Porn wasn't his only vice. They found your name on a list that we suspect are victims of his side hustle, blackmail."

She sat back. Perhaps putting space between herself and his words would make them less real. Didn't work. "What could he possibly blackmail me over?"

"We all have something we wouldn't want somebody else to find out about us."

She leaned forward and clutched his hand. "Not me. What about you? What deep, dark secret haven't you told me about? Are you already married? Got a love child in the wings? Taking bribes from crooked officials?" She laughed. "That's ridiculous."

"Then why is your name on that list?"

"Was it handwritten?"

He shook his head. "Morgan said they found it in a document on his computer."

"Anybody could have added it, trying to implicate me. I'm glad your commander is smarter than that."

"Don't give him too much credit. He was writing up an arrest warrant when he called me."

She gasped. "I can't believe it."

He squeezed her hand. "Well, sure seems somebody has it out for you."

"And that certain somebody has a deep reach. Knows what's going on in my life." Her hand went to her throat. Where the ring once rested. "If you hadn't called me to meet here, I mightn't have an alibi. I was going to the shop. Wednesday mornings can be slow. At least here, a dozen people can say they saw me."

"Let's go to your place."

"Is that a good idea?"

"I want to check your computer and your phone."

"What for?"

"To prove you didn't contact him."

She looped her arm through his as they exited the store. "Is that wise?"

"You're right. I'll call in a computer forensic officer to do that. Don't want anybody alleging you had the opportunity to delete evidence because of your connection to me." He grinned at her as the dogs bounded ahead, yipping and yapping at the end of their leads. "We are still connected, aren't we?"

"I hope so." She bumped her hip against his, sending him off kilter. "At the hips and the lips."

"Never heard that one before."

"Grandma Carly says Grampa Mike used to say that about them." Her own cell phone beeped. She didn't recognize the number. "Hold on. I'd best get this." She leaned back against her car and pressed the CALL button. "Hello?"

"Yeah, this is Mike Woods. Where's my car?"

"I'm sorry, I don't understand—"

"I parked it at that lot next to your store. Signs say some company XYZ—"

"EZ Riders Towing."

"Whatever. Towed it away. Called them. They said they don't have it. Never took it. Never got a call to take it. So I figure you stole it."

"Mr. Woods, I am not a car thief." She glanced up as Ed's brow pulled down. Goodness, she'd already been charged with involuntary manslaughter and murder. Now grand theft auto, as well? "I called the company on Monday. They assured me the car would be towed because it was parked in my lot illegally." She paused. "That was two days ago. Why are you only now calling about it?"

"Had a bit of a binge and stayed over at my girlfriend's there in that Podunk town."

She shrugged. "Well, that's a private lot. It's posted as such. The car was gone shortly after. If you believe it's been stolen, call the police." She met Ed's stare and raised her eyebrows. "Did you go to the towing company and check their lot? Perhaps it's not processed through their system yet."

"Guy on the phone gave me an address, but when I got there, it was an empty field. When I tried to call again, no answer. What are you up to?"

"Nothing, Mr. Woods, I assure you." Ed quirked his head toward the door, and she nodded, then handed him her keys. "Look, I'll make a call and get back to you, okay?"

"Likely story."

She stared at her phone after he disconnected until Ed touched her arm. "What's going on?"

"A guy who parked in my lot without permission. He didn't even apologize for his rude behavior. And now

105

he says he can't find his car. The towing company is giving him the runaround. He thinks I took it." She sighed and held out her hands. "Maybe you should lock me up right now."

"Got enough paperwork already. Don't need any more. Check with me in June." Ed held out her keys, which she accepted. However, instead of releasing them, he used them to draw her close, then kissed her, sending off fireworks in her heart and head. "I like your grandmother's motto. Let's adopt it as our saying, too."

Our saying. Has a nice ring.

Alarms went off in her head, warning her to take it slow with him. She didn't want to cause him problems now or down the road with his career. And she sure needed no more heartache if it turned out they never worked their way back to more than friends.

She put distance between them. "Careful, Detective. Heaven forbid somebody should see you fraternizing with a suspect."

"Nonsense. The only thing you're guilty of is stealing my heart."

{*}

On the drive back to Margie's, Ed glanced in the rearview mirror, noting his grin. He'd best wipe that off when he next saw the commander. A quick call ensured a forensic technician would meet them at Margie's to check her phone and computer.

Bruno panted in the back seat. "I know how you feel, boy. I'm glad to see my sweetheart, too."

While there would be no opportunity for the two neutered dogs to produce pups, romance might still bloom between them. Until they went their separate ways into training as guide dogs for the blind, that is. The thought caused a tinge of sadness, which Ed shook off. Dogs didn't feel love the same way people did.

Did they?

Margie led the way and pulled into the parking lot at the store ahead of him. After parking, she released JoJo, who danced when Bruno emerged. They went upstairs, all four, and the pups settled down with doggie treats while Margie retrieved her computer and set her phone on the counter.

Ed wanted to look at both devices but refrained. "I want to be able to say, in court, if necessary, that I never touched either of these."

They didn't have long to wait. At a knock at the side door, Ed went down and returned with a young woman in casual clothes, sporting a police vest and hauling a briefcase on wheels.

He introduced her. "Carol Cook, meet Margie Hanson."

A curt nod, then she went to the purpose for her visit. She glanced at him. "Did you—"

"No, ma'am, I didn't."

Officer Cook looked at Margie. "True?"

"True."

Another nod. "Good. Won't take me but a couple of minutes." Her fingers poised over the keyboard.

"Password?"

"Bearcove. One word."

The officer's fingers flew, and she nodded. "I'm in."

Ed wanted to watch over her shoulder but restrained himself. Better he knew nothing about the contents of the computer or the phone.

About twenty minutes later, Officer Cook snapped her case shut. "Nothing on either device. I'll write up a report to that effect."

After the forensic technician left, Margie made them coffee, and they relaxed in the living room. "So, I'm out of the woods on this case?"

"Insofar as electronic or digital contact is concerned, yes.

Her brow pulled down, marring her usually placid expression. Seemed he'd seen that look far too often in recent days. Maybe he could put this behind them and remedy that. "Maybe Elgin contacted you in other ways?"

"Such as?"

He sipped his java. "In person or at the shop."

"Like in the movies? On a train? A plane? A shared cab?"

He chuckled. "Now you're making fun of me."

"Well, thankfully, I've not been to any of those places recently. Plus, I have no reason for a sleazy porno king blackmailer to extort money from me. As if I had any." She brightened. "I could provide bank records."

"That would help. Although you operate a

business with cash coming in all the time. Morgan might argue you paid him that way."

She shook her head. "All sales go through my register. Less than ten percent of sales are cash. All accounted for."

"Maybe you siphoned it off the top."

She growled. "Whose side are you on?"

He held up a hand. "Just sayin' what others might think."

"What can I do?"

"I believe you. Remember that. In fact, maybe you can help me. If you promise to keep a low profile and do what I say."

She studied him. "I see."

"You do?" He wasn't sure he did. Not like he had a plan or something. "How so?"

"I can see what married life will be like. Me barefoot and pregnant in the kitchen, obeying your slightest whim."

Was she serious? What kind of man did she think—he detected a twinkle in her eye and her lips twitched. She was having him on.

Well, two could play at that.

"Exactly."

Her eyebrows shot up.

"Not."

She giggled, which alerted the dogs that play time had arrived. The two pups jumped on the sofa between them, licking whatever exposed skin their tongues could reach. It took him several minutes of wrestling and laughing to get the pair under control and settled on the floor again.

Margie swiped her hair from her forehead. "Well, if this is what life with you will be like—"

"Yes?"

"Maybe, at some point, you can count me in again."

He leaned over and kissed her. "Nothing is easy with you, is it?"

Chapter 10

Thursday morning, while Margie braved an unexpected bout of freezing rain as she walked JoJo around the lake, she wondered if she'd made the right decision with—or rather, about—Ed. After all, while she obviously hadn't killed this man Elgin, she wasn't out of the woods yet regarding her court cases.

While she had uncanny connections to the first two deaths, this new killing must be linked. Surely a town as small as Edgewater wouldn't have two, or even three, killers on the loose at the same time?

As she rounded the final turn in the path, the wind bit into her skin, smashing ice pellets into her nose and mouth. Glad she'd worn a scarf, she tugged the edges up to form a barrier, then paused and squatted, using her body as a windbreak for the dog. "Hold here, girl." She patted the Lab's head. "I know. It's hard to see and breathe, isn't it?"

She glanced around. Apart from a couple of benches facing the lake, there was no protective cover in this area. She could walk to the southwest corner where the restrooms and a maintenance shed huddled, but that was three more blocks.

She stood. Home to the warmth was best.

She tugged on the lead. "Come on. Let's quick-trot it back."

JoJo yipped then bounded ahead, pulling Margie along the now-frozen path. The dog's nails scrabbled for hold, while Margie slipped and slid, trying to keep her balance. "Slow down. Not so fast."

Thankfully, obedience classes had paid off, and the pup stopped at the crosswalk until the light turned in their favor and Margie gave her the command to walk forward. The painted stripes seemed even more slippery than the bare asphalt, so she took extra care crossing.

A few more blocks, and the parking lot came into view. No cars other than hers. Which reminded her of the rude Mr. Woods and his missing car. Had she—and he—been victims of a scam? She sighed. All she wanted was to turn back the clock to last week and have her application approved. Show the town she was here to stay. Invest. Improve the downtown area.

She shuddered. The last time she'd thought about that, Earl Cramer was alive and well. Was she cold and crass for thinking of her business while the man lay cold and dead?

It wasn't like she knew him personally. Although perhaps a little compassion for his family was in order.

Inside the house, she wiped the dog's feet with the towel hanging from a hook, then released the canine, slipped off her boots, and headed toward the stairs. As they passed the door to the bookstore, JoJo paused, nose in the air.

Margie peered around. "What do you hear? Or

smell?" Margie sniffed the air a couple of times. Something faint, like chemicals. Paint? "Come."

She unlocked the door, the dog leading the way, then paused in the doorway. The retail area looked secure. Door shut and bolted. Glass intact. But something on the windows obscured her view onto the street.

Using her hand, palm facing the floor, she gave JoJo the *down* command. The dog obediently flopped to the floor, chin on front paws, eyes on her. She crossed to the door, unlocked it, and stepped out.

Across the plate-glass window, in blood red paint, one word: KILLER.

She glanced up and down the street. Still too early for other shops to be open for business. The street quiet. Nobody in sight.

Margie touched the edge of the K with a forefinger. Still tacky, which meant the vandal visited recently. While she was out? Or maybe while she walked the hallway inside.

A shiver ran up and down her spine. Thinking somebody so vindictive would choose to vandalize her property cut her to the quick.

And scared her.

Inside the shop, she locked the door, then called Ted, her handyman and Mr. Fix-It. "Can you remove spray paint from glass?"

"Usually. Depends how long it's been there."

"Less than an hour, I'd say. Still tacky."

"Oh, this is a current problem. Thought you

113

might be asking for information's sake." He chuckled. "Sorry. It's not so funny from your point of view. I'll be right over."

After she disconnected, she headed upstairs to fortify herself against whatever was coming down the pike next. Seemed not only the Edgewater cops had it out for her.

{*}

An hour later, Margie unlocked the front door of her shop once more. Ted had finished cleaning off the paint, and now gave the windows a well-deserved cleaning with a bucket of soapy water, a long-handled brush, and a squeegee.

One of her favorite customers, Mrs. Comerford, waited on the step. She smiled at the older woman and held the door open for her. The matron, dressed in her finest winter coat with the mink collar, nodded. "Wanted to show my support for you. I know you didn't do what they're saying."

"Thank you. I appreciate that." Margie's eyes blurred, and she wished others thought the same way. Oh, well. At this rate, she had at least four people who knew she was innocent: herself, Ed, Mrs. C., and the killer. Or killers. "What can I help you find?"

But the Mystery event display already held Mrs. Comerford's attention. She held up the first book. "What's this one about?"

"A man is shot. Sherlock Holmes helps find the killer."

Her customer giggled. "Ooh, I love anything with Sherlock." She snatched up the second. "Or Poirot. I've already got this one. A woman is poisoned, right?"

Margie waggled her hand near her mouth as though holding an imaginary stogie. "Give the woman a cigar. Right again." Something connected in her brain. Shooting. Poison. She picked up *The Big Sleep*. Another shooting. Along with pornography and blackmail. Just like the killings here in Edgewater. She glanced around. So far, Mrs. C. was her only customer. "Excuse me. I need to make a call."

The woman smiled. "No worries. I see you've replenished the markdown table. I'll simply amuse myself there."

After her customer selected an armload of books and carried them to an easy chair, Margie headed for the cash register desk and dialed number one on her speed dial. "Hi Ed. Listen, I was just talking with a customer, and something she said made me think about these cases."

"Can't talk right now. This evening, maybe?" Muffled voices in the background, then he spoke again. "Sorry. At work. See you at seven."

The phone went silent.

Snap. She should have thought about that before calling. After vowing to herself that she'd not jeopardize his job or his career, she'd perhaps done that very thing.

A shout from outside drew her attention. Ted brandished his brush over his head like a sword. "Get away before I call the cops."

The door burst open, and the lady from the bakery across the street hurried in, cheeks flushed and hair disheveled. "Goodness me. You're gathering quite a crowd out there."

Margie peered out the door. "What?"

"Seems you've riled up the fringe element."

"What are they saying?"

"One or two want you to close the shop and leave town. Permanently. Two old guys are suggesting a lynch mob would do justice."

"What did I ever do to them?"

"Nothing. They just need a cause." The woman thrust a folded bundle of newspapers toward her. "Didn't know if you got the paper, so I brought mine from the past few days."

Margie accepted the offer. "Thanks. I'll look at them when I get a chance."

A pat on her arm brought comfort. "And I'll catch up with Mrs. C. over there."

Back at the desk, Margie perched on the stool and opened the Monday paper, scanning its contents. Not on the front page, at least. In fact—she flipped several pages before locating her photo in the lower margin along with four paragraphs about Earl Cramer. While the article mentioned her name, accolades concerning Cramer's life and career took up most of the space.

Tuesday's paper contained the story of the mayor's demise, this time with Joan Young's picture instead of hers, which was fine with Margie. At that time, a brief statement from Commander Morgan revealed investigations were ongoing and a person of interest was in custody.

Margie snorted. Person of interest, indeed. More like only suspect.

Today's edition included a short piece about Bart Elgin's murder. This time, no mention of her.

Shooting. Poison. Another shooting. Head of a committee and a mayor. Could be considered lord and lady of the manor. And blackmail and pornography dovetailed completely with the third book and murder.

Was somebody copycatting her book event with these three murders? If so, who was next?

She picked up the next book. A body—or six—in a church? Or was this about the mode of death?

If so, suffocation awaited the next victim.

{*}

Promptly at seven, Ed pulled into the lot at Margie's shop. He parked and exited, a bouquet of grocery store flowers in his hand. Not a peace offering. Friendship only. That's all he could ask of her right now. Anything more, and she'd resist—maybe even run. And he wouldn't blame her. If their situations were reversed, he'd distance himself as much as possible, so the allegations did not stain her reputation.

When she called earlier, his heart raced, and his palms sweated at the sound of her voice. But the stern countenance of Commander Morgan sitting across the

117

desk from him curbed his delight. Had his superior figured out who was on the other end of the call? If so, he didn't mention it. Didn't admonish or warn him. Instead, the man carried on discussing the administrative tasks he'd assigned instead of investigating the recent murders. Busywork, Ed called it. Essential to smooth operations, the commander assured him.

He rang the bell, and Margie released the lock from the intercom in her apartment. Perhaps if Great-Aunt Roselda had spent a few dollars and installed one like it, she wouldn't have died. He shook his head as he trotted up the stairs. No, that would only be true if her death were accidental.

And, if not for the older woman's demise, he'd never have known Margie.

Or her wacky grandmother, Carly.

The younger woman whose face rarely left his mind waited at the top of the stairs, smiling down at him. Her eyes widened when he offered the flowers. "How lovely."

"The lady at the floral counter assured me they were friendship flowers."

"Then they are doubly lovely." She turned away. "Let's go in the kitchen while I get a vase." She pulled a pale blue round-bowled container from a cabinet. "Would you like coffee?"

"Decaf, if you have it." So far, so good. She seemed at ease. Hospitable. Chatty. Just like the old Margie. "I can make it while you fix the flowers."

"Sure." She filled the vase and added plant food, then cut through the plastic and released the stems by snipping the elastic. Next, she measured the length against the depth of the vase, cutting each on an angle before tucking it into the vase. A couple of twitches, the greenery, and she was done. "There." She held the arrangement aloft. "What do you think, JoJo?"

The pup woofed, and Ed laughed. "She says you missed your calling."

Margie's very kissable lips pursed. "I guess if I lose the shop, I could start a new career."

Despite her jovial tone, Ed recognized the serious tone. "No worries about that ever happening. Folks here love your shop. And you."

"Not everybody, apparently." They carried their cups to the living room and sank into her old sofa while she told him about the vandalism and the protesters outside the shop that morning. When she finished, he patted her hand. "Just some kooks. Did you make a police report?"

She shook her head, shoulders slumped. "Don't know if you've noticed, but the cops and I haven't been on the best of terms lately."

"I did sense that." He sipped his coffee. "When you called this morning, you said you had something to share. I'm all ears."

"You know I'm doing that Mystery Book event for December, right?"

"Uh-huh."

"So I have four books, each by different authors, different settings. I brought in current reprints so customers could afford to purchase them, keeping the vintage editions on display and adding a few bits for setting."

"How is it working?"

"Hard to tell. Sold a couple of books today. Then again, I only had two customers brave enough to come in." She waved off the problem. "But my first customer asked for a mini-synopsis, and I realized there is a similarity between the books and the killings."

Unsure he really wanted to know, still he had to ask. "How so?"

She held up a hand and counted off on her fingers. "First book, lord of the manor, shot." Another finger up. "Second book, lady of the manor, poisoned with strychnine." Third finger. "The next, a blackmailing porno shop owner, shot."

"Coincidence?"

"Sure, the first one, maybe. But strychnine is an unusual poison. Difficult to get hold of. But one I had here in the shop. Nice for planting evidence against me."

"And the third victim bears an uncanny resemblance to a specific character type, while his mode of death isn't."

"Right. So, it seems somebody is following my book event. Except they didn't know I'd have an alibi for the third killing. Probably thought I'd be alone in the shop all day. Not out canoodling with a copper."

He leaned close. "Is that what we were doing?"

"Not really. I was going for the alliteration."

He'd rather canoodle. "So, what's the fourth book about?"

"Glad you asked." She picked up a book from the coffee table. "*Hawksmoor*. It's set in two time periods. Current, at least as of when the book was published, early 1970s. And the origin of the mystery, two hundred years prior. An architect murders a series of people to sanctify the churches he's building, and a handsome detective looks for a serial killer in his time who is murdering people and leaving their bodies in churches."

"How did he kill them?"

"Strangulation or suffocation."

"Well, thankfully, no deaths that way. Yet." He peered at her. "A handsome police detective, did you say?"

"Right. That was the fiction part."

"Really?"

"Really." She stared at him, her mouth working to keep from smiling. "The big question is how we can catch this guy."

"Poison is a woman's weapon, remember."

"True, but female serial killers are rare. Like, almost nonexistent."

"You're probably correct that it's a man. But which part of *we* includes you? You're supposed to keep a low profile, remember?"

She pouted, her bottom lip sticking out in a most

adorable manner. "But I can't sit by and let somebody railroad me into prison." She rubbed her upper arms. "Or worse."

And neither would he. He'd keep an eye on this woman who'd stolen his heart from the first time they met.

And then he'd make certain to steal her heart.

For good, this time.

Chapter 11

Friday morning, Ed arrived at the station, fresh coffee in hand, which he set on his desk. As he removed his outer coat, his desk line rang. He snatched up the receiver. "Hogan here."

Scratching and rustling on the other end confirmed somebody held the phone and kept the line open. Perhaps trying to decide whether to speak? Or what to say? An amateur, perhaps. Or a lie. Lying doesn't come easy to most people. Folks tend to stammer over the untruth.

"Hello? This is Detective Hogan. Edgewater Police. How can I help you?"

"Better get out to that killer's bookstore. She's done it again."

Margie? He breathed deep and exhaled to calm his racing heart. Best to play dumb for now. "Which bookstore is that?"

A sound like a growl. Or a snort of frustration. "You cops don't know what's going on in your own town? She's killed again, I tell you. Listen carefully. Body. Alley."

"What's the address?" Was his caller simply an early morning spook? Crank caller? Or something more nefarious? "And why aren't you calling 9-1-1?"

"Because you'll want to be on scene and arrest

your girlfriend again. I'm looking forward to it. And this time, she won't be walking the streets like a normal person. She's dangerous and needs to be locked up for the rest of her life." A mirthless chuckle filled Ed's ear. "Or worse."

The call ended, leaving a buzzing of dial tone like a hive of angry bees awakened from their winter's rest. He replaced the receiver and sat, sipping his coffee.

He couldn't very well ignore the call. The man— and he was fairly certain the caller was male despite efforts to disguise the voice—said enough so Ed knew Margie's store was the reference, and it sounded like he'd be in the crowd of onlookers, since he referenced his enjoyment at watching Margie's arrest. If he didn't show up and at least act as though this was serious, the man might well leak the story to the press. Which would put both Margie and him in a poor light, not to mention the entire Edgewater Police Department.

He shrugged back into his coat, picked up his now tepid coffee, and headed for the door. As he passed the desk sergeant, he tossed a wave. "Got a call about a body behind the mystery bookstore. I think it's a crank call, but gotta check it out."

"Want me to send a patrol car instead?"

Ed hesitated. This wasn't a call for service he'd normally take, but the caller seemed intent on making it personal. And if it involved Margie in any way—even if only that someone dumped the body on her property—he wanted to be there. No matter what Commander Morgan said. "Sure. Send a car. If I need forensics, I'll call it in."

The desk sarge called out to the nearest patrol car, then turned back to a stack of paperwork with a grunt. "Probably a false report. Stay safe out there."

Ed tapped the imaginary brim of his non-existent cap and left the building. Within minutes, he pulled into the parking lot. He turned when a car with a powerful engine squealed to a stop, then turned into the lot beside him. Good, first on scene was a rookie just out of training.

The officer, fit and lithe from police academy training, parked the car, then trotted toward him, acknowledging him with a nod. "Detective. Sarge said you have a body?"

"Thanks, Miller. Might. Caller said it was in the alley." He led the way around the back of the building. "Not really expect—"

He stopped. Froze, actually. The rookie bumped into him from behind, knocking him off balance. Ed bit off a sharp retort, then pointed.

Propped up in a sitting position against the dumpster, a leftover Halloween decoration. At least, that's what it looked like from here. A pumpkin rested where the head should, like a macabre version of *Legend of Sleepy Hollow*. Except, in this case, the body wasn't headless. Or carrying its noggin under an arm.

He gestured to Miller to walk around the far side of the display, giving the immediate area a wide berth. "Don't want to mess up the crime scene. If it's a crime."

The young man grinned. "That's a pretty big if, sir. I'd say somebody is having a joke at our expense."

"Maybe. But if it's not, I don't want our clodhoppers muddying the waters."

"Understood."

They arrived at opposite sides of the body, and both knelt for a closer view.

Miller, his face pale, spoke through clenched teeth. "Looks real to me. But I've heard they make these lifelike mannequins now." He stretched out a hand to touch the shoulder. "Feels real. Cold."

Ed nodded, then laid a forefinger along the jugular. "No pulse. If it's a real person, they're dead." He scanned the position of the form. "Get some pictures before I remove the pumpkin. I have to do that to confirm it's real."

Miller pulled his cell phone from his pocket while Ed directed the shots he wanted. Then he instructed the rookie to take additional photos of the alley area, including wide angles of the body. If that's what it was.

When the officer moved away, Ed removed the pumpkin. Seeds and pulp from inside fell to the ground in a sticky morass. He set the gourd aside and swiped at the head, clearing the eyes, mouth, and nostrils.

Miller reappeared at his side. "Sir? Shouldn't we call in the coroner and forensics?"

Ed stared at the features of the woman at his feet, then stood. "Yes. I know her. It's Margie Hanson." He gestured to the building. "She owns this bookstore."

"Isn't she the one—"

"Yes. But this time, the caller got it wrong. He said she killed this person. Ironic, isn't it? Trying to lay the blame on the victim herself."

While Miller called in the death, Ed made a couple of calls of his own.

{*}

Half an hour later, Ed stood before a group of reporters. "Thank you, folks, for coming out on this chilly morning. I wanted to update you on what happened here today. No point in letting you run with your own version of events, because we all know you'll just make it up as you go along." He chuckled to prove he was kidding. "Seriously, a woman has died. While we have not released her name pending notification of next of kin, suffice it to say she is—" His voice broke, and he cleared his throat. "Was a resident of the town."

A reporter from the town weekly raised a hand. "Can you confirm if it was Margie Hanson, owner of the mystery bookstore?"

The ring of journalists and media pressed in closer, microphones and digital recorders raised to get the best sound bite.

Ed shook his head. "As I said, no formal identification yet."

The same gangly young man persisted. "Has family been notified?"

"We're in the process right now."

"How did she die?"

"Strangulation and then suffocation from inhaling pumpkin pulp and seeds is the initial assessment from the coroner, pending a full autopsy."

A well-known local news anchor, Lisa Bailey, stepped forward, her nails and lipstick perfectly matched. "Do you think this death is connected with the previous three?"

Ed smiled to himself. That was the question he'd hoped somebody would ask. "While our investigation is ongoing, I believe this death now raises the strong possibility that the same person killed all four."

A radio talk show host raised a hand. "Do we have a serial killer on the loose? And if so, should we be worried?"

"I wouldn't call this person a serial killer. More like a cowardly copycat, hiding behind the skirts of a woman. He is mimicking the plots in a series of books. I've consulted the psychological crimes unit of CBI— Colorado Bureau of Investigation. They've told me we're likely looking for a male, fifties, socially inept, probably mentally unstable, who sees his crimes as a holy crusade of some kind."

Ms. Bailey peered at him. "Do you believe these crimes are religiously motivated?"

"Not by any conventional faith system. Only by the deranged confusion of a man without boundaries, who thinks that his reasons are enough to end the lives of four citizens of our town." He glanced up at the windows of Margie's apartment. "If you'll excuse me."

Most of the reporters took this as their cue to return to their stations and papers to write their story. The gangly young reporter and the well-manicured Lisa Bailey, however, hung about, asking questions of onlookers. Ed surveyed the crowd, but no single face stuck out as out of place or unnaturally curious. Still, he couldn't be too sure, so he nodded to Officer Miller, who lounged against the building. The man nodded and took stills and video of the crowd as Ed had instructed him previously. They'd check back at the police station for anything—or anybody—unusual.

Using a key Margie provided him the last time she was in jail, he let himself in and went upstairs, returning a few minutes later with JoJo. The dog danced on the end of her lead, planting her paws on his legs.

He patted her head. "Good girl. Yes, I know. Margie isn't here right now. Let's go see Bruno." He loaded the pup into his car, where she settled on the back seat, tongue lolling. Then he sat in the driver's seat, door open, and spoke to the canine. "No worries, girl. You'll always have a home with us. It will be one way for me to keep Margie alive."

At movement beside the car, he turned. The news anchor. She made a point of turning off her recorder. "Off the record, Detective?"

"What?"

"I know you foster guide dogs for the blind. Is JoJo in the same program?"

"She is. Not a good guard dog, though."

"Why do you say that?"

He stepped out of the car, and Lisa took a couple of steps back. "You know the story, don't you, about what's really going on here?"

Up close, she looked older than on camera or from a distance. Tiny wrinkles around her eyes and mouth, masked expertly with makeup and shadowing, testified against her youthful appearance otherwise. "Been on the job a long time, Detective. It is Margie Hanson, isn't it?"

He nodded.

"And you and she were in a relationship?"

"Still off the record?"

She crossed her heart with a forefinger.

"We were. But then she was accused of murder, and I had to step back." He inhaled, then breathed out deeply. "I told her I believed she didn't kill anybody. I hope she knew that—at the end."

"I suspect she did. And she understood." Lisa patted his forearm. "Will you keep me updated? I'd like to be the one to break this story. When you're ready."

He tossed her a half-smile. "You're on my speed dial." He locked the door. "For now, I need to put up a sign in her shop and make certain I secure the premises."

After closing the blinds of Margie's apartment and hand-lettering a sign indicating the shop was closed for the immediate future because of a family emergency, he locked the door behind him.

The clicking of the deadbolt mirrored the sense of

a door closed forever in his heart.

Would he ever get over this?

{*}

Upstairs in her apartment that evening, Margie huddled under the blankets, wishing JoJo was with her instead of having a fun time at Ed's with Bruno. Then again, if she really wanted to maintain this subterfuge, she mustn't draw attention or give anybody any sign she was alive.

Lavender shampoo—and plenty of it—finally removed the smell of pumpkin pulp from her hair. She'd probably never eat another pumpkin pie in her life. She shivered, cold on the inside although toasty warm on the out. Making the call to the police department, knowing it would be recorded, without laughing and giving away the plan, was one of the most difficult things she'd ever done. Brought to mind her Grandma Carly's stories of waiting in her own house for the killer to make a move on her. And then doing the same in the hospital, while Grampa Mike and the police chief hid in the bathroom.

Well, that turned out fine, didn't it? No reason to think it wouldn't this time. Although she worried that Ed might have poured on his loathing for the killer a little too thick. What if the man saw through their plan?

She might well end up posed in the alley for real tomorrow if that were the case.

Anticipating a long night of worrying, a bump from downstairs came almost as a relief. Perhaps they'd get this over with sooner rather than later. Near the door leading to the parking lot, another bump, then the tinkling of breaking glass.

He was on the move.

Time to get into position.

She slipped out of bed and padded to her office and computer. After repositioning the furniture that afternoon so she sat with her back to the door, she turned on the laptop, added her noise-canceling headphones, and sat. Humming along with imaginary music, she waited.

The soft shuffling of footsteps on the stairs. The squeaky one at the top. A long pause as the intruder waited for a reaction.

She shrugged back her shoulders and lifted her hands to the keyboard as though working on a document. Oh, snap! Open one. Word processing program launched, she randomly typed nonsense words, remembering to hit the space bar and the hard return key occasionally. No point in this failing to work because her actions weren't realistic.

A hand covered her mouth and nose, blocking off her breathing. Well, she hadn't exactly expected that. Clawing at the fingers, she wrested her way out of his grip.

Silhouetted against the glow from the streetlight, a man faced her, his face in shadow. While his identity was in question, his words and motivation weren't. "I'll kill you for sure this time, woman."

She stepped back, her hands raised in front of her. "I don't think so."

"Think what you like. I won't fail."

When he approached, hands like claws aimed at her throat, she screamed.

Two dark forms erupted from the kitchen and tackled the man, who ended up on the floor on his stomach, face pressed into the carpet. While one man held the intruder, the other—Ed—flipped on the lights. She scurried to his side and pressed against him.

The other man—Officer Miller—snapped on handcuffs and yanked the intruder to his feet. Still screaming obscenities, the man blinked and gave each the evil eye.

Ed pulled his detective shield from his pocket. "Ed Hogan. Edgewater Police. Who are you?"

Slathering at the mouth, the man sneered. "Carl Stanley. Not talking to you or anybody else. Don't have to. Know my rights."

Ed grunted. "Well, we'll see about that."

He withdrew his cell and dialed a number while Margie sat in her computer chair again. Now that the excitement was over, her knees were a teeny bit shaky.

After a brief conversation with somebody at the station, Ed turned back to them. He quirked his head toward the man in custody. "Carl Stanley here filed a missing person's report twenty years ago. Seems his wife disappeared. Went to the grocery store and never returned. So he says."

Margie's brow rose. "And she's never turned up?"

Ed shook his head. "So, Mr. Stanley, got anything to say for yourself now?" Miller cleared his throat. "Yes,

Officer?"

"Should we read him his rights?"

Ed sighed. "You're correct. Don't want him getting off on a Miranda technicality. You do it."

The young officer pulled a pre-printed, laminated card from the chest pocket of his uniform and read aloud the admonition that anything Mr. Stanley said while in custody could be used against him. "Do you understand your rights, sir?"

"Perfectly."

"Do you wish to answer question related to your conduct tonight and any other cases or investigations we might consider pertinent?"

"I did it." Stanley held his chin high as though proud of his accomplishments. "I killed her. Buried her under the parking lot. Well, it wasn't a parking lot then, you know. The old lady who owned the store and lot wanted it paved. I underbid everybody else so's I'd have a place to put the body where nobody would ever find it." He laughed as though this was the greatest joke in the world. "That crazy old coot paid me five hundred bucks. Heck, I'd have done it for free just to get my old lady out of my life."

Ed jotted down notes in a small book from his pocket. "And what about Earl Cramer, Joan Morgan, and Bart Elgin?"

Stanley peered at him. "In for a penny, in for a pound, me old nan used to say. Cramer and Morgan, they were easy. Don't like bureaucrats and couldn't take the chance they'd approve her renovations."

Recognition dawned on Margie. "You're the man I talked to about redoing the lot after I completed the building. I couldn't figure out why you didn't want the job."

"Yeah, thanks for alerting me to your plans." He sneered. "That was a piece of luck, let me tell you. Couldn't have you digging up the past." He hung his head. "Gotta bury the bad."

Seemed poor reason to kill three people. And try to kill her. "But how did you know about the books?"

"Mrs. Comerford is a neighbor. She mentioned the display. The first two were pure luck."

Ed shook his head. "And Bart Elgin?"

"He figured out what I'd done. Been paying him off for years. When she told me about the third book, seemed the time was right to get rid of that minor problem, too."

Ed nodded toward the door, and Officer Miller took hold of the suspect just above the elbow and directed him downstairs and out of the building.

When the side door closed, Margie exhaled and stood. "Coffee?"

"Only if it's decaf. I'm still hoping to snag a few hours of sleep tonight."

"I feel bad that my book event enabled him to kill those people."

He followed her to the kitchen, then lounged in the doorway. "It didn't. It simply provided a skeleton for him to hang his crimes on. He could just as easily have watched a true forensics or real crime show on television. Or read a book. Or gone to a movie. Ideas are everywhere. Some people use them for good. The evil use them for their own ends."

She brewed a couple of cups of coffee, one at a time, then set them on the table. "I guess you're right."

He cupped his ear with a hand. "Sorry. I don't think I heard that. Speak up."

She giggled. "Fine. You're right."

"Now we're off to a great start again." He sipped, then set his cup down. "Seriously, I know how you feel. Every time I give a talk in a school, one kid is bound to ask me about my most exciting case. Or the one I never solved. And I always wonder if I'm giving them fodder for the next Great American Novel or for the unsolvable bank heist of the century."

"We really can't control what people do, can we?"

"Nope. And we only rarely talk them out of doing something wrong. That's why we need God in our lives. So we can hopefully speak some of Him into others'."

She yawned. "Good reminder, Detective."

He reached across the table and held her hand, which tingled at his touch. "Breakfast tomorrow?"

"Do you mean Saturday or Sunday? Because it's already past midnight."

He laughed. "Saturday. At the Dew Drop Inn?"

"Sounds like a plan. I can walk there. I'll need the fresh air to clear away the cobwebs."

He brushed a lock of hair back from her face. "You're beautiful, spider gossamers and all."

She forced an exhausted smile. "You're well read. Sounds like you hang around somebody who owns a bookstore."

"If that's what happens, then I hope to become the most eloquent person around."

"Is that a promise or a threat?"

"Take it any way you like."

Chapter 12

The next morning—Saturday—Margie climbed out of bed, feeling more rested than she had in days. And so she should. After all, the police arrested and charged the actual killer the previous night. Or early this morning. She'd slept straight through once her head hit the pillow, no longer worrying about another death being blamed on her.

Was it only a week since this nightmare began? Hard to believe how much circumstances threw her life into turmoil.

First thing on her list: call her mother and let her know that all charges against her were dropped. A text from Ed and one from her bail bond company already confirmed the truth—she was innocent.

She tapped her mom's picture in her favorites list, and her mother picked up on the first ring. "Margie? Are you all right?"

"Yes, Mom." She pictured her mother running fingers through her hair. "Wanted to let you know I'm off the hook. They caught the killer, and he confessed."

"Oh, honey, I'm so glad to hear that. Your father and I have spent hours praying that God would work a miracle."

"Well, He did. He also used Ed and a young

police officer to keep me safe and make the arrest."

"This sounds like we need a longer chat."

"We do, but not right now. I'm heading off to meet Ed for breakfast. You could keep that in your prayers, too."

"We will. Anything specific?"

How much to say? Maybe she'd blown this entire episode out of context. "I gave Ed back his ring because I didn't want him having to choose between supporting me or doing his job."

"What did he say?"

"That he believed I was innocent, but he understood."

"And?"

"Oh, Mom, I don't know what to do. If he asks me to marry him again, what do I say? I mean, what if something like this comes up again? After we're married?"

"Then God will take care of it again. Just like this time." A long pause filled Margie's ear. "I think you're more concerned he won't ask again, aren't you?"

She considered her mother's words. "Yes. How do we go on being friends if he doesn't trust me enough to marry me?"

"Is that what you think his failure or perhaps delay in asking will mean?"

"Doesn't it?"

"What do you think when you ask God for something, and you don't see the answer right away?"

Margie rolled her eyes. She knew where this was

going. "The answer might be *no*, or it might be *not right now*."

"And why is that, in either case?"

"Because it's not the best thing. Not His perfect plan."

"Would you want to marry a man who isn't walking as best as he can in God's perfect will?"

"No."

"Then trust that he hears from God. If you can't start there, you shouldn't marry him at all."

They sent their love over the airways and Margie promised to call again to talk longer. When she disconnected, she sat, the phone still in her hand, until JoJo whined.

"You're right, girl. Time to get this day on the go."

A quick shower, a double-time walk around Sloane's Lake, a treat when she settled the pup in her doggie bed, then Margie sauntered the two blocks to the Dew Drop Inn to meet Ed. Cars already occupied the spots along the street, and the parking lot looked full. She checked her phone. Two minutes late. Not bad. Hopefully, he had a table.

And if he didn't, they'd wait. Maybe in his car. The sun breaking through the morning overcast would warm them in no time. And they could talk. Clear the air.

In which case, she might return home and making her own breakfast.

The stroll along the main road helped her

organize her thoughts. Spend time in prayer. Give it all over to the One Who was really in control.

When she stepped inside the diner, her mouth watered at the scents of bacon, toast, coffee, and cinnamon buns. She searched the tables, spotting Ed in a far corner.

Bless him, Lord, for finding us a quiet place to eat and talk and get reacquainted. If that be Your will.

She waved and headed in his direction. But before she made it, a vaguely familiar woman stepped into her path. Margie stopped.

The woman smiled and extended a hand. "Lisa Bailey. Channel 10 News. Congratulations on being completely exonerated of all charges. And rightfully so, I might add. I never believed the evidence against you. I mean, thinking a librarian could kill somebody. Sure, if it was about overdue books or dog-eared pages."

On autopilot, Margie returned the gesture. "Um, thanks."

Lisa leaned closer and lowered her voice. "He never stopped believing in you, no matter how it looks. He's a keeper. If he was twenty years older, or I was— well, never mind. I think we both know who owns his heart."

Lisa sat and continued her conversation with her tablemates, while Margie turned toward Ed again. Several other diners nodded in her direction. Another stood and shook her hand. The attention made her feel like a celebrity, which, as she thought about it, she was. In a way. From notorious cold-blooded killer to assisting police solve four murders and close a cold case regarding a missing woman. All in one fell swoop.

She slipped onto the bench seat across from Ed, then exhaled. "Whew. That kinda felt like running the gauntlet."

"Only in a good way."

She nodded. He hadn't shaved this morning, although judging by his slicked-back hair, he'd showered. She recalled the smells that clung to her hair and skin after a night in the cells. Did he notice the same thing? Was there a police-strength body wash for getting rid of those peculiar odors? Maybe someday she'd ask. But for today, for now, she'd let him set the tone and direction of their conversation.

Their server, Barbara, appeared, pen and order pad in hand. "Know what you want this morning?"

Margie turned her mouth down. "Not a clue. What's good?"

"Everything, but my favorite is the breakfast burrito with sausage, smothered in green chili."

Her mouth screamed yes. "Sounds good. Hash browns. Coffee."

"Gotcha." Barbara swiveled to face Ed. "You?"

"Same."

A quick x2 on the notepad, then she returned in less than a minute with a carafe of coffee and a bowl of creamers. Margie poured for both of them, then doctored her java while Ed did his own.

Margie quirked her head back toward the crowd in the diner. "Did you put Ms. Bailey up to that little stunt?"

He peered at her over the rim of his cup. "What do you mean?"

"Oh, I don't know. Semi-famous local TV personality just so happens to have breakfast in our little diner. Recognizes me. Stands up and pronounces me innocent as a newborn babe in front of the movers and shakers of said community. Seemed a little staged."

"Nothing to do with me."

"You didn't make a call or send a text suggesting we might be here?"

His eyes widened, and he jabbed his chest with a forefinger. "*Moi?*"

She laughed. "You sound like my Grandma Carly."

"Good to know we have something in common, she and I. She's a wonderful lady."

"That she is."

"Have you talked to her since this all started?"

"No, but I'm sure Mom has." She sipped, then set her cup down. "So you didn't put Ms. Bailey up to saying what she did as a personal aside, either?"

He shook his head. "No idea what you're talking about."

If she couldn't believe him about this, what did that say about their future? "This coffee is wonderful."

He clapped a hand on the back of his neck. "Ooh,

whiplash at that change of subject. What did she say?"

She lifted one shoulder and let it drop. "Nothing important."

He set his cup down and reached across the table. She left her hand where it was, and he intertwined his fingers into hers. "While we have a few minutes, I wanted to say again how sorry I am that my job interfered with our relationship."

"There wasn't anything either of us could do about that. And I wouldn't want you to lose your job or advancement opportunities because of me."

"But don't you see that all of this made me realize how important you are to me?"

No, she hadn't. Well, yes, she did. He'd put everything on the line to keep her updated, to include her in the plan to catch the killer, and to keep her safe. Setting up that ploy to aggravate Carl Stanley into doing something stupid was brilliant. Playing his part so skillfully they'd even fooled the media was brilliant.

Or maybe only most of the media. Lisa Bailey seemed to have him pegged.

Margie nodded. "And I'm sorry that my plans to expand the shop put that pressure on you and jeopardized your career and our relationship. I love you, but I completely understand if you're second-guessing our future together. Maybe we need more time to figure out how to handle situations like this in the future."

He peered at her, rubbing her thumb with his. "Sounds like you expect something to happen." He leaned forward. "What are you planning?"

Another chuckle. "Nothing. But Grampa Mike says my grandmother is a full-time job with a nose for mystery. In more trouble than she's out. I expect I take after her."

Ed sat back and dug into his pocket, then held out his hand, palm up. Something glittered, and she gasped. Her ring. "I have learned not to doubt what God brings together."

Her mouth went dry, even as her fingers itched to snatch the diamond from his hand before he changed his mind. She hesitated and locked her gaze with his. "And if something like this happens again?"

"Unlikely, but if it does, it will be more difficult to give back the ring once we're married. So, I'm opting for a brief engagement to make certain we tie the unbreakable knot. If you'll have me."

Have him? She'd marry him today if she followed her heart. But that might not be best. She swallowed hard, then folded his fingers to enclose the ring within his fist. "I'd like to think about it—for both of us." His gaze dropped and his shoulders slumped. Not what he'd expected. Or wanted. But her mother's words echoed in her head. She must be certain. "Let's both pray for God's perfect timing on this."

He nodded. "Fine. I'll give you all the time you need." A half-grin lit his face. "So long as it doesn't take longer than today."

"Can't promise that. But to occupy your time and

energy, there is something you can help me with."

He groaned. "Oh, no. You're starting already with the mysteries?"

"Sort of."

Barbara arrived at the table bearing their plates of food and another carafe. "Hot coffee." She nodded to each. "Anything else?"

Margie nodded. "Yes. Do you know who holds the contract for towing here?"

"Sure. ABC Towing. Great company. Quick and careful. Even the folks who get towed say they're easy on their cars and don't charge a lot. Why?"

"Ever hear of EZ Riders Towing?"

Their server's mouth turned down. "Don't use 'em. Bunch of crooks. Cars disappear. Probably shipped to Mexico."

"Any idea where I might find them?"

"There's a junkyard at the end of 26th and Jay. I heard they take a sledge to the cars to disguise them."

After thanking her, Margie and Ed devoured their breakfasts. Ed because he was a growing boy, or so he declared, and Margie because she was ravenous.

Nothing like a little mystery to perk up the appetite.

{*}

Ed parked his car about two blocks from their destination, then he and Margie stepped out. Sure enough, a sign on the eight-foot metal privacy fence bore the name of the business: EZ RIDERS TOWING AND

PARTS.

He met her on the sidewalk. "So, remember. I'm the cop here, not you. The one authorized to make a search if I see anything suspicious. You stay behind me, right?" She nodded. "But until that time comes—if it comes—we're here to buy rims for my car. Somebody jacked it up last night and stole them, tires and all. That's our cover story." Another nod. "Okay, let's go."

They strode toward the corner and in through the gate. Business hours indicated somebody should be on the premises. They stopped and looked at a couple of sedans on their way in to bolster their subterfuge.

A man in overalls came out of a mobile home converted into an office, if the sign on the door was correct. "Hey there. What kin I do fer ya?"

Margie tugged on his sleeve. "That's the man on the phone. I recognize his voice."

"Ssh." He addressed the fellow who looked like neither he nor his clothing had been washed in recent months. "Looking for rims."

"Name's Jared." He held out a hand. Ed shook it, then swiped his hand on his jeans when the man looked at Margie, who wisely kept her hands in her pockets. "Where's your car?"

"In my driveway on blocks." He went through the horror and disbelief of finding his car vandalized. Jared nodded his way through the tale like one of those little bobbing dogs on the dashboard that were so popular during his parents' time. "So, I need four rims."

"Make and model?"

Ed and Jared continued their conversation while Margie tagged along. Pleased with how well she followed his instructions, he shadowed Jared until they reached the aisle supposedly containing vehicles similar to his own.

But when he turned around, she wasn't in sight.

He growled. "Women. Never want to make it easy for a guy, do they?"

Jared grunted. "Can't live with 'em. Can't live without 'em."

Ed made a mental note to strike this man off his list when seeking sage advice. "Honeybun. Where are you? Don't get lost."

A muffled reply proved she was at least still within earshot. "On my way, Sweetkins."

Jared chuckled. "Sounds like you got her well-trained."

"Oh, she is." Ed lowered his voice. "Just don't say anything about it in front of her. She can be a little touchy."

The junkman smiled. "Love a touchy woman."

"Well, she's mine." He nodded toward a car with all four rims intact. "Will those fit?"

"Let me check."

While Jared scanned a barcode on the inside of the driver's window, Ed spotted Margie beckoning to him from the aisle opposite. He waved. "Be right there, Honeybun." He glanced at Jared. "I think she got mud on her new shoes and expects me to clean it off for her."

148

Jared chuckled. "Dames."

Ed trotted to where he'd seen Margie, but she wasn't there. He looked left and right, shrugged, and chose left. About twenty feet along, he heard her voice.

"Oh, what a nice car. I wish my boyfriend would buy me a black Lexus like that. Show me some respect, you know."

What was she up to now?

He rounded the corner. Margie stood with her back to him, facing three men and a semi. The back end of the semi was open, revealing at least three high-end sports cars, including the one she'd told him about that EZ Riders towed from her parking lot.

He slowed, tucked one hand into his jeans pocket, and slouched forward as if out for a stroll. "Hey, Honeybun. What'cha doing?"

She glanced over her shoulder and nodded toward the truck. "Just telling these nice gentlemen how I'd love if you'd get me a car like that." She turned back to the three. "Is the black one for sale?"

"No." A skinny guy with scraggly blond hair and a goatee backed away from her. "I mean, it's already sold."

She stuck out her bottom lip. "Oh, but I like that one. Can I look at it?"

A burly older man with grizzled hair stepped in front of her. "He said it's sold, lady."

She waggled her head from side to side. "Well, o-kay."

Ed gripped her arm. "Honeybun, let's not bother

these men, right?"

"But you said you wanted to buy me something nice."

"I was thinking more along the lines of a leather coat, not a luxury car."

One hip jutted out, and she pulled from his touch. "Oh, is *that* how much you love me?"

He raised both hands. "No, no, no. That's not what I meant." He turned to the three, who now grinned back at him, arms folded across their chests. "Can you help me out here? Please sell me the Lexus."

The third man, pimply faced and overweight, shook his head. "No can do. As he said, that car is on its way to—"

"Shut it!" The older man stepped forward. "Where's Jared? What are you really doing here?"

He reached inside his jacket, but Ed was quicker. In a flash, his duty weapon trained on the three. "Edgewater Police. Drop your weapons."

Three handguns and a wicked-looking knife thunked to the ground. He kicked a nine-mil in Margie's direction. "Watch them."

Her brows raised, disappearing beneath her bangs, but she picked up the weapon, clicked off the safety, and leveled it at the suspects. "With pleasure."

Jared called down the aisle. "Hey, man, those rims won't fit. Sorry. We ain't got nothing in stock that will." He sauntered closer. "I can take your number and call you when—" He froze when Ed pivoted, gun pointed at him.

"Holy—"

Using his weapon to show Jared should join his friends, Ed waited until the man stood beside them, hands raised, before pulling out his cell phone and calling Officer Miller. 'Yeah. Ed Hogan here. Bring backup out to the EZ Riders' junk yard." He listened a moment. "It'll be the collar that will make your career." He filled the rookie in on where to find the suspects and the stolen cars. "I think at least one of these yahoos will roll on his buddies." A glance at Margie to make sure she was still okay. Calm and steady. Like a pro. "No, we won't be here. This one is all yours."

Margie glanced at him. "You're giving this to a rookie?"

He snorted. "I don't need the collar. Or the paperwork. Help me tie them up."

Using the two sets of restraints attached to his belt, he cuffed them together and to the door of the Lexus. "Seems only fitting we should shackle them to the car."

"I'm just glad I found out what they were really doing before too many cars went missing. I felt so bad when that guy called and said his car was missing."

"Well, maybe he'll be more careful whose lot he parks in."

She smiled. "There is that."

Sirens sounded in the distance. Ed nodded to Margie. "Let's make ourselves scarce." He grabbed her hand and led her out of the yard and to his car. After they buckled in, he turned to her. "Where to now?"

"How about my place?"

Oh, how sweet that sounded. They weren't out of the woods yet, but she had thrown him a life saver.

{*}

Back home again, Margie stalled for time. She'd not had much time to consider Ed's re-engagement. No opportunity to pray. Still, they worked well together. Both loved the Lord, were avid readers, and he was certainly a man she could envision spending the rest of her life with.

But after turning down several offers for coffee, tea, or water, and assuring her he wasn't hungry, Ed peered at her for a long moment. "I get the distinct impression you're trying to put me off."

She sank onto the sofa beside him. "Not exactly true. But sorta."

"Sorta?" He frowned. "Should I leave?"

She laid a hand on his forearm. "No. I want you to stay. I think."

"You think? If you're not certain—"

She sighed. How to explain? "As I said before—"

"You're worrying about something that may never happen again."

"But if—"

"If it did, we'd get through it. And if it didn't, you'd have wasted your life." He slipped to the floor on one knee and held out the ring again. "Which would you rather?"

She held out her left hand, and he slipped the ring

on her fourth finger. She moved her hand from side to side, catching the glint of the light on the diamond. "It's beautiful."

He sat beside her again. "Not as beautiful as you." He kissed her, raising a longing deep within her. Then he moved apart. "But there's one more thing you'll need to add to your calendar over the next couple of months. Besides the engagement party on Monday, that is."

"Oh?"

"Yes. I want to enroll JoJo in several basic training classes at the police academy."

"So she can chase down the bad guys?"

"No, silly. So I never have to worry about you being unprotected. I couldn't stand it if something happened to you."

She mock-punched his arm. "And there was you suggesting nothing like this would ever happen again."

"I don't think it will. At least, I hope not. But as the granddaughter and grandniece of two feisty women, I expect lots of situations in our long married life."

"You think so, do you?"

"I do."

Now it was her turn to boldly kiss him. Which she did. Then she held him at arm's length. "Keep those two particular words handy in your repertoire, Detective Hogan."

"Why?"

"Because you'll barely have time to catch your breath after the party on Monday and I'll be walking down that aisle to meet you."

"I'm looking forward to that."

"Me, too."

A massive weight lifted off her shoulders, and she glanced heavenward. God had just answered her prayers, letting her know beyond a doubt that marrying Ed was the absolutely best plan. Sure, she expected situations. After all, He never promised them they wouldn't have troubles.

Nothing is easy—not in love. Or faith. But with God in control, well…

She had nothing to worry about.

THIS MIGHT BE THE END OF MARGIE HANSON'S ADVENTURES, BUT YOU CAN LOOK FORWARD TO MORE GREAT STORIES IN THE FUTURE.

About the Author(s)

Donna lives in Denver with husband Patrick. As a hybrid author, she writes squeaky clean historical suspense and contemporary suspense. She previously published contemporary books under her alter ego of Leeann Betts, but now authors books in her name only. She has been published 50 times in novellas, full-length novels, devotional books, and books on the writing craft. She is a member of American Christian Fiction Writers, Writers on the Rock, Sisters In Crime, Pikes Peak Writers, Christian Women Writers, Faith Hope and Love Christian Writers, and Christian Authors Network; facilitates a critique group; and teaches writing classes online and in person. Donna also ghostwrites, edits, and judges in writing contests. She loves history and research, traveling extensively for both.

STAY CONNECTED...

www.DonnaSchlachter.com Sign up to earn about new releases, preorders, and presales, as well as check out featured authors, book reviews, and a little corner of peace. Plus: Receive a free ebook simply for signing up for our free newsletter!

www.DonnaSchlachter.com/blog

Check out previous blog posts at www.HiStoryThruTheAges.wordpress.com and www.AllBettsAreOff.wordpress.com

Facebook: www.Facebook.com/DonnaSchlachterAuthor

Twitter: www.Twitter.com/DonnaSchlachter

Books: Amazon: http://amzn.to/2ci5Xqq

Etsy online shop of original artwork: https://www.etsy.com/shop/Dare2DreamUS